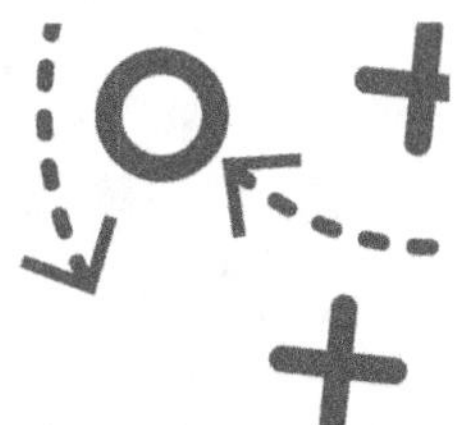

BEAUTIFUL GAMES

To all the dirty girls.

SAN DIEGO SOL WELCOMES ELEANOR BIGSBY AS CONDITIONING COACH.

San Diego Sol Football Club: For Immediate Release

A recent graduate of San Diego State University, Bigsby looks to improve the team before the upcoming MLS season.

San Diego, CA, January 16- With the approaching season, Executive Vice President of Soccer Operations, Maxwell Bigsby, turns to family to strengthen the players, not only on the pitch but behind the scenes as well. Ms. Bigsby will join the team, effective immediately, serving as an integral part of the San Diego Sol's technical roster.

"I am elated to welcome Eleanor to the San Diego Sol family, not only as the EVP of operations but also as a proud father, who has delighted in watching his daughter grow into her own."

The San Diego Sol joined Major League Soccer in 2018 and continues to bring world-class athletes to spectators from around the country.

END RELEASE

I STARE at the press release tacked to the team bulletin board before tearing it from the cork. Crumbling the flimsy paper between my fingers, I fling it into the nearest trash can while loudly exhaling into the near-empty locker room.

Fucking Bigsby.

Sure, the guy owns the team I've been playing for since their inception–and sure, we came in second-to-last in the league last year–but what does he hope to accomplish by hiring his daughter?

Eleanor Bigsby. Even her name pisses me off.

Cole strides into the room, his British accent thicker than my own, as he speaks. "I see the big man hired us a new babysitter."

In the often-inconsistent world of professional football–soccer to Americans–Cole has been an almost constant presence in my life. We grew up together, just outside of London. What started as a friendly competition between two over-confident boys on the pitch quickly morphed into a partnership as we realized how formidable we could be when we worked together–me, a striker, and Cole, as winger.

Going our separate ways, we climbed through different teams in lower-level leagues before reuniting in the top-tier English league where we played a glorious two years together.

We won championships together. We celebrated together. We partied hard together, being dubbed the Bad Boys of Blackpool before one *tiny* incident with a group of rowdy strippers and a table full of drugs had our faces plastered over every tabloid in the UK.

Hell, living up to that bad boy image wasn't easy. But we sure as hell did.

Quickly, the partying overtook us. Nights out in the beds of beautiful women became more important than early morning workouts. We slipped on the pitch, causing our team to lose important fixtures–or games, for the non-soccer inclined. Our mates stopped trusting us to do our jobs. Our coach was decidedly fed up with playing clean-up to a "duo of tattooed, hard-headed playboys" –his words, not mine.

As anyone could expect, when our contracts were up, neither of them were renewed.

Instead, we were sent to separate lower-level teams, fighting for minutes on the pitch, fighting to stay relevant in the league as we aged past our prime while younger and younger players continued to claw their way into the space we had carved out for ourselves.

And then, the unthinkable happened. We were relegated even further–to the MLS. Where the best of the best–myself and Cole included–come to die.

Well, maybe not die, per se, but definitely where once world-class caliber football players came to retire. And like many that came before us, that choice wasn't entirely our own to make.

I had bills that needed to be paid; parents and siblings who relied on me for financial support. Sure, I had some offers for coaching, or worse yet, commentating, but I didn't want to coach or give play-by-plays as younger versions of myself ran around the pitch.

I wanted to fucking *play*.

So, here I am, almost past my prime at thirty-fucking-four.

Playing in a league often laughed at not only by people who enjoy football but by players from leagues around the world, too.

You know how the saying goes, "at least we have each other."

Well, at least Cole is here with me, silently rotting away as we chase what could be our last season as players–our final attempt to prove that we've molted that bad-boy image, that we've reformed ourselves into something profitable, something that can be marketable to fans and our community, something that might be worth taking a chance on when our playing days are done.

Snapping back to the present at Cole's voice coming from behind me, I stop my internal jog down memory lane.

"Let's go, brother." He claps a hand on my shoulder. "Last Friday before full practice starts, and I know *just* where to go to spend it."

Okay, so maybe we haven't entirely shed that bad-boy image, but hey, I've always found that the ladies love a bit of a rebel.

SEVERAL HOURS AFTER THE SUN HAS SET, I FIND myself alongside Cole and several other members of our team. We're huddled around a small VIP table on the third level of City Syn, an upscale nightclub and favorite spot for high-powered businessmen. Swapping stories from our pasts and not-so-distant previous conquests, we chat as the sounds of laughter from nearby tables drift around us much like the sounds wafting up from the DJ spinning beats two floors below.

The club is lowly lit, dramatic uplighting lining the walls as strobes flash below us. The lights and strobes mix with a light fog piped in across the dance floor to create an almost villainous atmosphere–the perfect place for dark and dirty deeds. Assorted, deep-purple couches flank the VIP area, a thick velvet rope blocking the space from the rest of the club as well as from the throngs of people hoping to catch a glimpse of the table filled with professional athletes. Men wanting to be us and women wanting to be with us look on from afar, and it's not lost on me that more than one beautiful woman tries to bypass the wall of muscle standing guard at the rope.

Maybe it's about time that I stake my claim on one of those lucky women–for the night, at least. I'm not the forever type of man, but I sure as hell don't mind having a nice piece of ass to warm my bed from time to time.

Moving from my group of friends, I walk to the railing that separates the VIP section from the rest of the club below, watching the bodies on the dance floor two levels down as they move along to the heavy thump of the bass. The floor looks alive in a collision of limbs and torsos, and as the crowd cheers at the start of a new song, the throngs of people almost seem to meld into one giant body moving in unison.

A group joins the floor, and my eyes immediately lock on the sexiest woman I've ever seen. In a sea of rack-thin bottle blonds, she stands out in the crowd as her fire-engine red hair cascades around her face in wild ringlets, stopping midway down her back. This broad has curves with a capital C, and they... are...*glorious*. My fingers tingle, aching to pull her body flush with mine, to hold onto those luscious hips. She's not trying to hide in the background, not trying to slink away and blend in with her surroundings. No, she wants to be seen as she moves to the music, tossing that wild mane around as she dances to the house beats without reservation.

Walking to the burly man in charge of the rope, I nod in silent thanks as he lifts it, allowing me to pass as I leave my friends behind. Quickly, I make my way down the two flights of stairs to the main level in search of the captivating redhead who doesn't know yet that she'll be coming home with me tonight.

It takes me a few minutes longer than I want, stopping multiple times to take several selfies with fans. As always, I dutifully smile for them, knowing full well that if it weren't for my fan base, I would have likely been on a plane back to the UK after my first season here.

Still, I'm happy when I reach the first floor and find that most people are too preoccupied with gyrating on one another or their groups of sloppy, drunk friends to notice me as I look around the room, searching for Red in that sexy little leopard-print dress.

I'm scanning the dance floor, searching for her wild hair when movement catches me off to the side. She's at the bar, drink firmly clasped between her hands as a handsy man steps closer and closer to her. What was only moments ago a free spirit, a woman free from inhibition, she now stands ramrod straight, an apparent scowl marring her pretty face.

Well, fuck.

My feet propel me across the room in several long strides, and I don't stop until I'm standing directly behind her, my chest dangerously close to pressing against her unassuming back.

It's louder on this level than up on the third floor, but I can just make out the man trying to convince the firecracker to leave with him. "Come on, Elle. It'll be good for us. Give us a chance to reconnect."

I take another step closer, so close that if I inhale deeply, my chest will be flush with her body. Handsy dude's eyes finally leave her face to land on mine. "Woah," he says, getting ready to blow my cover, "are you…"

I cut him off before he can continue. "No one; I'm no one, mate. And from what I can ascertain, the lady would prefer it if you were no one as well."

Without another word, he glances at the woman one last

time before he scurries away from the bar with his tail between his legs. Finally, Red turns toward me, and I'll be damned if she isn't even more heavenly this close to me.

Piercing green eyes are heavily winged with thick, black eyeliner and equally dark lashes. Her little dress is painted to her curves like a second skin, dipping tantalizingly low in the front while pushing her full tits together as if on display.

I have to shake myself before I dive in and motorboat those beautiful suckers right here at the bar. Hell, it wouldn't be the first time I've done that, either.

She stares at me as I continue my not-so-subtle perusal of her luscious body, all the while holding onto her empty glass as if it is her own personal life raft.

Time to turn on the charm.

Holding out my hand to her, I wait patiently before she concedes, her dainty hand sliding into mine. "I do hope I was not being too forward–Elle, was it?"

She nods hesitantly, not speaking.

I continue, "You see, Elle, I've been watching you from upstairs, and if I'm being completely honest with you, I could not take my eyes off of you."

I reach up, brushing a wild curl behind her ear. Her eyes widen, but she doesn't pull back, doesn't make any attempt to escape our one-sided conversation.

Gesturing to her empty glass, the same one she has been white-knuckling for the last few minutes, I proposition her. "Allow me to buy you a drink. I'd love to grab a quieter spot with you outside on the verandah and get to know the woman who has captivated me."

Her cheeks flush under my simple words, and after a moment of hesitation, she agrees, her voice huskier, deeper than I expect. "Do you mind if I just tell my friends real quick? I don't want them to worry about me."

I flash her that megawatt playboy smile of mine, the one

known to make women throw their panties at me. Again, it has happened more than once. "Beautiful Elle, you don't have to ask me for permission. I would never want you to feel like you were being put in a position that made you feel anything less than safe. Go–tell your friends. I'll order our beverages, and you can meet me right back here."

I gesture to the bartender and wait for our drinks as Elle crosses to the still-full dance floor, her beautiful curls bouncing and hips swaying with every step.

Placing two drinks in front of me on the bar, a scotch for me and a vodka cranberry for Elle, the bartender waves off my payment. "Man, I'm a huge fan. Sure you guys will have a better season than last. These two are on me."

I exchange pleasantries with him before dropping a fifty into his tip jar, turning just in time to see Elle rejoin me.

Lifting up her glass, I make to pass it to her, but she hesitates before speaking. "How can I be sure you didn't slip something in my drink while I was gone?"

One, I'm not that kind of man, and two, I want her more than alert for what I plan on doing with her body later, but I sure as shit won't be telling her that. Instead, I settle for a simple, "I can understand how that could be something a beautiful woman like yourself would have to be concerned with, and I apologize on behalf of the entire male species for that. I can assure you, I mean you know harm, but let me put your mind at ease."

Flagging down the bartender once more, I explain the situation to him and wait as he quickly makes Elle a new drink, placing it directly in front of her on the narrow bar top. She smiles, thanking him profusely before pulling a card that has been tucked somewhere in the depths of her dress. As he previously did with me, he waves the payment away, and I'm sure to tuck an additional twenty into his tip jar as a sign of thanks.

Maneuvering us through the crowds, my hand firmly placed

against her lower back, we exit to the verandah. We claim one of the small cocktail tables as the water cascading from an ornate outdoor fountain gurgles against the music seeping into the outdoor seating area.

We sit side-by-side, and she takes a minute to study me, not speaking, simply taking in my form. I can tell from her gaze that she appreciates my athletic physique as her eyes rake up my corded forearms, bare of the dress shirt that I've rolled up several times. Just a hint of ink is on display, peeking out from my right sleeve, but I can see her eyes working to uncover exactly what is permanently scribed on my flesh.

"I can't help but feel like I'm at a disadvantage," she finally speaks after what feels like minutes of silence.

I bring my glass to my lips, allowing the Macallan to slide down my throat while I choose my next words. "And why is that, beautiful Elle?"

Her cheeks flush, but not nearly enough to match the color of her hair before she continues, "You already know my name, but I still don't know yours."

I tuck the same unruly curl behind her ear, bending in slightly closer to her. "And a beautiful name yours is."

From the short interaction we've shared, it's apparent she doesn't know of my near-celebrity status and my proven track record of debauchery. And for once, I'd like to keep it that way. She doesn't give off the air of being the type of woman who would go home with me, strictly based on my name and reputation, so I decide to keep my cards close to my chest. Giving her a long-standing family nickname, I extend my hand, much as I did several minutes ago in the bar. "You can call me Jay."

She slightly stutters, nerves apparent as she softly clasps my hand in hers. "Ja...Jay, nice to meet you."

Pretty young thing she is, I decide to not push her too quickly. "I do hope I didn't overstep at the bar before. It looked as if the gentleman was bothering you."

Elle gives me a small smile, one that doesn't quite reach her eyes. Nonetheless, it is stunning, just like the rest of her. "No, I appreciate you stepping in. Jonathan doesn't know how to take no for an answer."

Sipping gingerly from the tiny cocktail straw in her glass, her cheeks hollow as she pulls in the liquid, and I can't help but think of what those cheeks would look like hollowed out, her lips around my cock. Releasing the straw, she locks eyes with me. "And do you know how to take no for an answer?"

I bark out a deep laugh. "I guess that depends."

"On what?"

I think for a minute before answering. "If I asked you to dance with me and you said no, I'd respect that. But, if I was lucky enough to get you in my bed and you said 'no' when I asked you for one more delicious orgasm...well, I certainly don't know if I would take that no for an answer."

She sucks in a deep breath, her chest rising and falling heavily. It's not lost on me that her pupils suddenly dilate, and when she exhales, a simple, "Oh," is the only word to whisper across her lips.

We're locked in a battle of eyes for several long seconds. Neither of us talking–simply her green eyes staring back at my own baby blues. She hasn't run yet though, and that's a solid indicator that she's not as easily scared as I expected her to be.

Placing my now empty glass on the small table between us, I reach for her hand, pleasantly surprised when she doesn't pull away. "Dance with me?"

"And if I say no, you'll drop the question. Just like that?"

My gut churns. I want this woman in my bed tonight. But I won't be a complete ass about it.

"Just like that," I respond.

She stands and starts to walk away, that tousled mane bouncing with every step, and I'm momentarily stunned that she is simply walking away from me. Women don't do that. Women don't fucking walk away from Jensen West.

I'm almost ready to bolt from the verandah, to take my wounded ego back upstairs to find a willing jersey chaser to take home with me for the night. But then, Elle turns around.

"Well, you coming or what?"

And with that, she walks back toward the inside dance floor with me closely behind.

Reconvening on the dance floor, I take my place behind Elle as she sinfully moves her body in time with the beat of the music. Not wanting to draw attention to myself–this moment belongs fully to her–I gently sway back and forth, letting the music course through my body.

The light fog caressing the dance floor floats up around us, appearing to make her even more confident. Suddenly, she is facing me, slowly roving her hands over my chest as she lowers her body towards the ground before working her way back up my torso as if I am her own private pole.

Elle brings her arms up, resting them around my neck before she closes the distance between her lips and my ear. Speaking over the music as she continues to move her sinful hips against me, her words jump through my body and straight to my cock. "I would never say no to multiple orgasms from you, Jay."

Fuuuuuuuuck.

Walking her backward until her back is flat against the nearest wall, I cage her in with my hands before dropping one, allowing it to run down the slope of her neck and across her collarbone before tracing down the deep vee of cleavage between her breasts.

My mouth is fucking watering, and unable to resist any longer, I close my lips over hers, trailing my hand back up over her skin and into the wild curls of her hair. Instinctively, she moans into the kiss and opens for me, allowing me to delve into her mouth with my tongue. I explore her mouth like it is a lost treasure, taking what is mine. Every kiss, every nip and lick, Elle is right there with me, taking what she wants as her own in the low light of City Syn.

I break our kiss, my lips mere centimeters from hers. "Tell me, Elle. How much have you had to drink tonight?"

Her breath is warm against my lips as she speaks. "The one you bought me and one other. Why?"

I grind my hips into her, letting her feel how hard I am for her. "Because I'm going to ask you to come home with me, and I want to be sure you aren't making that decision under the influence."

Hell, I might only be a one-night stand kind of guy, but I would never take advantage of a woman who was intoxicated.

"Ask me." She all but purrs the response.

I tilt her chin, so she meets my eyes with hers before placing a sensual kiss on her lips. She looks up at me through hooded eyes, her lashes fanning out beautifully against the creamy color of her pale skin. "Come home with me for the night, Elle."

She takes her plump bottom lip between her teeth. "Lead the way."

Outside, we hop into an Uber, and a short time later, we're pulling up in front of my house.

Well, it's really more of a compound.

Situated to overlook the Pacific, the mansion boasts stunning ocean views from almost all rooms of the house and features direct beach access–a rarity in this area. A custom home theater, wine cellar, and chef's kitchen–all of which rarely get used–were just a few of the features that sold me on the property. I wanted the house to be a retreat. A place my parents and siblings could come to escape their lives–not that any of them have taken me up on the offer.

Did I go a little overboard when I bought it as a single man?

Sure.

Was it worth it when I got to watch Elle's eyes widen as we pulled into the circular drive?

Absofuckinglutely.

Her adorable little stutter is back as she speaks. "You...you live *here?*"

I hold open the front door, ushering her inside. "Home sweet home, Princess."

Elle turns to face me, a sly grin on her cute lips. "Jay, somehow, I doubt you're the type that plays Prince Charming."

She's fucking right about that.

Without warning, I scoop her up, tossing her body over my shoulder. She squeals as I lay a smack across her backside. "Sweet Elle, I might not be prince charming, but I'm certainly ready to introduce you to my dragon."

She laughs as I carry her over my shoulder to the primary suite which occupies an entire wing of the house. A giant four-poster bed sits in the middle of the room, a small seating area off to the side, and enormous floor-to-ceiling glass windows showcasing clear views of the ocean. There is a separate patio off the room, and after placing Elle's feet gently on the floor, I open the door to the patio, allowing the late-night sounds of the waves to serve as our backdrop.

Turning back to Elle, I find she is already behind me. She runs her hands up my chest, working each button on my dress shirt before sliding it off me. Slowly, Elle runs her fingers over the smooth skin of my chest, over the swirls of ink that covers one of my pecs before trailing up over my shoulder. "Tell me what you like, Jay."

It's not a question–more of a quiet demand–and damn if it doesn't make my dick even harder than it already was. This vixen is so willing, so eager to please. If it were any other woman, I would find it a turn-off. But not with Elle–not with her wild green eyes and equally chaotic hair.

"Rough, Princess. I like it rough."

Without waiting for her to respond, I'm on her, pressing my hips into her soft flesh, grinding against her as I fuck her mouth with mine. My hands run through her hair, and I pull my mouth from hers long enough to pull her hair back, exposing the column of her neck before nipping and sucking my way down to the swell of her tits where I adorne her silky skin with love bites.

She whimpers as I knead her tits through the fabric of her dress, all while keeping my other hand firmly tangled in her hair. When I bring my eyes back up to meet hers, almost all of the green of her eyes are gone, in its place, two dark obsidian orbs of lust.

"Woman, if I don't get this fucking dress off of you, I'm going to go crazy."

Her eyes are defiant, blazing. "Then take it off me."

There is no more time for idle chat as I divest her of the dress. I follow the fabric as it slides down and pools at her feet where she quickly kicks it to the side. I take her in, starting at her feet, where perfectly manicured toes peek out from sky-high fuck-me-heels. Toned calves lead to powerful, thick thighs, and I can't help but picture her squeezing those thighs around my head as I tongue fuck her pussy while she writhes on the mattress beneath me.

A simple, black thong covers her sex, the slightest bit of soft skin spilling over from its constricting fabric. I want to bite at it–to leave marks on the soft flesh of her stomach.

As hard as it is to pull myself from the spell her magical pussy has me under, my eyes continue upward, past the hour-glass figure her hips create, over the belly button that I want to flick my tongue over.

I expect to find a matching bra, perhaps something lacy and black, but I'm stunned when I find her completely bare. And *fuck*, her tits are magnificant.

Alabaster skin fades into dusky pink nipples, already hardened by the combination of ocean air flowing into the room and her arousal. Easily the largest natural tits I've ever been privy to, I want to alternate between lapping at her nipples with my tongue and sliding my rock-hard cock between them before cumming on her pretty little face.

"Fuck," I grit out between clenched teeth. "There is *so* much I want to do to you, Princess, but if I'm not inside your cunt in the next minute, I might go mad."

Tease that she is, she simply widens her stance before flashing a coy grin in my direction.

I should take her to the bed, but I don't. Instead, I back her to the windows overlooking the ocean until her back is flush with the glass. The innate sense to claim her has me going wild, and I'm almost disappointed that the beach in front of my house is private because God*damn* would it be hot to have someone watch as I fuck this woman senseless against the glass.

I make quick work of my pants, not fully removing them, and only stopping long enough to procure a condom from my wallet. Moving to open the foil packet, Elle stops me with gentle fingers. "Let me."

She takes the packet and tears it open, letting the wrapper fall to the ground.

Then, without hesitation, she bends at her knees, takes my cock in her mouth one solitary time, swirling it around and making it nice and wet before releasing it. While maintaining eye contact with me, she slightly unrolls the condom, gingerly placing it between her lips before lowering her mouth onto me in one swift motion, unrolling the condom onto my cock as she takes my length in.

"Jesus fucking Christ, Elle. You are a dirty girl, aren't you?"

"And tonight, I'm all yours."

She's not even fully standing before I lift her, encouraging her legs to wrap around me as I slam her back against the glass.

"Jay, no, I'm too heavy."

I've got killer quad and glute strength thanks to hours of conditioning my body to be in top football shape. She's nowhere near too heavy, but I can't quite form coherent sentences right now to tell her that.

Instead, I squash any doubt by lifting her higher and sliding her thong to the side before sliding her onto my cock, impaling her in one fell stroke.

"Shiiiit," she hisses as I enter her in one movement.

"Too much?"

One of her hands leaves my neck, coming to pull the short hair atop my head. "Fucking. Move. Jay."

And fucking move, I do. I slam into her again, and she cries out. Her bare ass checks are against the window, legs wrapped around my waist as I hammer into her over and over. The position, the angle, the penetration–it's fucking phenomenal and I have to silently count in my head to keep from busting right away.

Sliding out of her to give myself a moment of reprieve, I set her down, positioning her now with her chest to the glass. Elle drops her head, but I fist her hair, bringing her face parallel with the window while my other hand snakes around her hips in search of her clit. Finding it, I rub several light circles around the already swollen bundle of nerves, and I swear I can feel her pussy flutter beneath my ministrations.

"Imagine if there were people out there, Princess. Imagine strangers watching you in here, those luscious tits pressed up against the glass, your own arousal leaking down your thighs. Would you like me to take you in front of strangers, Elle? Would it turn you on to be claimed and fucked and degraded with eyes on you?"

Her breathing picks up, chest heaving as I keep her pinned between my own solid chest and the wall of glass.

"Oh, God, yes!" she moans as I resume running my fingers

through her sopping wet folds. "Claim me, Jay! Fuck me and treat me like a filthy slut."

Christ.

I pinch her clit, causing her to scream, before all but dragging her to a nearby armchair. Folding her top half over the arm of the chair, her ass taunts me as she sways her hips. Smacking her ass, I watch as a handprint blooms across that tempting, ivory skin before sinking my cock balls deep into her tight, tight pussy. "You want to be treated like a filthy little slut, Elle?"

"Yes!" Her cries fill the room mixed with the sounds of our bodies slapping together. "Harder!"

My hips piston faster and faster as a sheen of sweat breaks out across my chest. "My little Princess is filthy. Tell me, should I let you cum before I explode all over your face?"

"Please, please let me cum."

Obliging her request, I fit my hand between her body and the chair, strumming her clit as I continue to mercilessly pound into her cunt. She is fucking *soaked,* and I can't get enough of the sound of her pussy sucking my cock back into her body with each thrust.

The first signs of her orgasm come as I feel her muscles constrict around me, her back arching, her moans echoing off the walls.

Several more thrusts and she's crashing over the edge, a guttural scream leaving her lungs as I wring every drop of pleasure from her body before she collapses lifelessly over the edge of the chair.

I continue to thrust, continuing to use her pussy as I chase my own release. "Did you change your mind, Princess?"

I fully expect her to say yes, for her to tell me to just get it over with and finish inside the condom.

"No." She pants the word through heavy breaths. "No, Jay. Mark me with your cum."

I groan as I pull out of her, instructing her to her knees. I pull out of the condom, not even caring that I drop it on the floor, before grabbing my cock and positioning it in front of her face.

Gloriously dirty woman that she is, she looks up at me through sated eyes, momentarily bites her lip, and then opens her mouth, gifting me her tongue in a silent offering.

And that is all it takes.

My balls tense as my own orgasm courses through my body. Spurt after spurt of thick, creamy cum coat her. It's on her face, on her lips, coating her tongue, and in her hair.

And she's never looked more stunning than in that moment, on her knees with my cum painting her face.

That is, until she takes a finger, collects the cum from her lips, and swirls her tongue over the digit.

She's a fucking sex goddess.

I help her off her knees, and not even caring that my cum is covering her face, I press my lips to hers, taking her in and loving the taste of myself against her tongue.

Helping her to the bathroom, I allow her a few minutes to clean herself up, smiling at her when she exits a short time later with a fluffy bath towel wrapped around her body.

I press another light kiss to her lips before excusing myself to the bathroom to do the same, all the while wondering if just maybe, she could be the one to break me of my one-night-stand-only rule.

Opening the bathroom door, I'm ready to ask her for her number, to ask her if I can take her out for a proper date. Only when the door swings fully open, my bedroom is empty, vacant of the firecracker that has already infiltrated my mind.

What the fuck?

Her dress is no longer on the floor, the towel she was wrapped in neatly folded at the edge of my bed, and the only trace of her is the Elle-sized ass print her body left behind on my floor-to-ceiling windows.

I cross the room to look out the window, letting out a long sigh as I stare at the dark ocean in front of me. Turning around to clean up my mess, something catches my eye on the ground, and when I bend to pick it up, I notice it's a credit card.

It must have fallen out of wherever she had it tucked into that dress.

This is good, I think to myself. I can use it to track her down, to ask why she ran.

I flip the card over in my hand, looking for her full name only to come to a standstill when I read the embossed letters on the bottom of the card.

Eleanor M Bigsby

Mother fucker.

What have I done?

PRESEASON PRACTICE TO BEGIN WITH FULL TEAM ROSTER REPORTING.

Soccer Daily Online: For Immediate Release

The full team roster has reported to Sol Stadium to begin conditioning for the upcoming season.

San Diego, CA, January 19- With the start of the season just a few weeks away, all players, coaches, and staff have reported to Sol Stadium for pre-season training. Along with several players joining the team from the San Diego Sol's soccer academy, the team has also expanded its roster with new signings in the off-season from Peru, England, and Brazil.

Owner Maxwell Bigsby states, "We are beyond thrilled to add such a strong caliber of players from around the world. Together, we hope to continue to bring the multicultural sport of football to America with top-tier athletes and coaching staff."

END RELEASE

SPRINTING down the hallway on Monday morning, I knock lightly on the door of my father's office before entering at his command.

Maxwell Bigsby may own the San Diego Sol, but he is rarely in San Diego. Actually, I can count the number of times I've seen my dear old dad in the last four years on two hands. But of course, on my first day as the new conditioning coach, he made it a point to be present. That's why I rushed to be on time. Hair still damp as it hangs around my face in wild ringlets, I give him a meek smile.

"Ah, Eleanor." His voice booms through his mostly vacant office. A few old, scattered, family pictures sit on a low credenza behind his desk, a wilting golden pothos in desperate need of water tumbles over the side of his desk, its leaves almost reaching the beige carpeted floor.

I take one of the two chairs across from his large, mahogany desk. "Dad, please, you know I prefer to be called Elle."

He scoffs, disregarding my request as he watches me pour most of my water bottle into his neglected plant.

He slides a paper across the desk and I take it, quickly glancing at the schedule set out before me, printed on branded letterhead.

9:30 A.M.- Facility Tour

10:00 A.M.- Meet Front Office Staff and Support Team
12:30 P.M.- Lunch
2:00 P.M.- Meet and Greet With Team and Coaches
Much like everything else in my short life, all the details are laid out for me, right there on a fancy piece of paper with the team's bright, embossed letterhead.

Go to school, get good grades, get into a good college, graduate top of your class, carve out an important and fulfilling career–in that order.

Here is the thing though.

My adoptive father might own this team, as well as have majority stakeholder rights in several other professional sports teams across the state of California, but I know *nothing* about soccer.

In fact, I've never even stepped foot in this building before.

Growing up, I was always a bit of a tomboy. I loved watching American football with my two older brothers. I dreamed of being part of an NFL team, even though that was unheard of at the time. I wanted to feel that camaraderie, to be part of a whole. I wanted to be on the sidelines during a game, helping to lead my team to victory in any way I could.

I decided to pursue a degree in exercise and nutritional sciences so I could do just that. I learned how to care for and treat minor injuries. Even more thrilling, I learned how strengthening and conditioning could prevent many of those same minor injuries that plagued big, burly professional athletes. And while I was putting what I learned into practice, my own body began to change, too.

What was once jokingly referred to as "baby fat" by my family slowly started to morph into some sort of pseudo-muscle. I still had soft spots that I knew would most likely never disappear, had thick thighs and a thicker stomach. I knew that I'd never look like the ideal athletic conditioning coach, but that was okay. I was determined to make my dream a reality and get to the NFL, slightly squishy tummy or not.

And then, Maxwell Bigsby happened.

My dad has always been a powerhouse of a man. From the time he adopted me and my sister, Michelle, he fully embraced us as part of the family. We were never treated as any less a part of the family than his biological children. He nurtured us from the time I was five, fully immersing us in the Bigsby way of life, pushing us toward our dreams, but always wanting us to find success on our own instead of on the back of the family name. He had given each child in the family a challenge upon graduation, and I was to be no different.

My sister, three years my senior, was now a chef at a popular restaurant in San Diego. But my father didn't simply hand her a restaurant upon graduation from culinary school. Oh no, that would have been too simple. Instead, he challenged her to work alongside a friend of his for one year–a friend who could only be considered the San Diego equivalent of Gordon Ramsey.

I lost track of the number of times Michelle came home over that year in tears, how many times she threatened to walk away, threatened to lock herself in the walk-in freezer and not come out, to quit, to move to a foreign country, or live her days off her trust fund while eating bread and backpacking her way around the world.

In the end, she toughed it out though. And now, she has a thriving restaurant of her own to show for the dedication and sacrifice she put into it.

The challenge my father was offering me wasn't much different from what he had offered Michelle. He was giving me the opportunity to fully immerse myself in a team culture, to build my own personal resume based on my love of athletic conditioning.

Only problem was, it was as part of a soccer team and had absolutely nothing to do with actual American football.

But it was only for one year.

I could do anything for one year.

Couldn't I?

Of course, I could! And at the end of this year, I would have real-world experience to my name. I would be able to take what I learned working for a professional sports team and apply that to the NFL.

Suddenly feeling reinvigorated at the thought of working alongside players and coaches I'd idolized for years when my tenure here was complete, I push up from the chair. "Are you leading the tour today?"

My father joins me in standing before making his way around the desk. "Yes. I thought it would be a nice way to start your journey here with Sol. It is the first day of training, but most training personnel won't arrive until this afternoon. That gives us an opportunity to spend some time together while you get acquainted with the building and facility."

Following closely behind, we walk through the open concept office space where several lines of cubicles sit empty. I can only assume that soon, the same cubicles will be filled with the people it takes to run an operation of this size.

It only takes a few minutes of traversing through the building before my father comes to stop in front of a large, metal door. Pausing with his hand on the doorknob, he turns to look at me. "I know this is different than what you would like to be doing, but I assure you, there is quite a bit of overlap between the worlds of American football and well, football. Keep your head clear, work hard, and I know you will reach your goals. In the meantime, welcome home, Eleanor."

Pushing the door open, he ushers me into the upper level of the stadium where we walk to a partition separating the owner's suite from the rest of the boxes.

It feels foreign and familiar all at once.

Taking in my surroundings, I bask in the glow of the sun as

it bounces off the metal stands, untouched by fans before the start of the season. The grass on the field is pristine as sprinklers sputter across the field, soaking it before our upcoming afternoon training session.

Across the upper seats of the stadium, S-A-N-D-I-E-G-O is spelled out in giant letters, the light blue of those seats standing out in contrast to the bright yellow of the rest of the seats in the stadium.

Quickly, I notice that this stadium is much smaller than any NFL stadium I've been lucky enough to visit. But still, even in its current vast emptiness, I can tell that when this place becomes packed full of rowdy soccer fans, it must be a site to see.

A thunderous voice booms through the stadium, causing me to jump back as my father chuckles. Turning and pointing to a large glass window far above where we are standing, he gives a wave to a man, an announcer, I guess, who bends back to a microphone in the glass box he sits in.

"Happy first day of training, Boss," the voice reappears. "Just checking out a few technical issues up here. Don't pay me any mind, sir."

Both my father and I turn back to the field, spending a few minutes in comfortable silence, taking in the gentle breeze that washes over the area. Finally, dad steps forward. "Come, Eleanor. I'll show you the rest of the concourse, and then we'll swing by the team store before I introduce you to the rest of the front office staff."

By the time we make it back to my father's office, I have an armful of team swag from the merchandise store. Everything from lanyards in team colors and San Diego Sol car decals to hats and even an embroidered blanket.

I'm introduced to a lovely woman who turns out to be my father's secretary, several of the sales representatives who reside in the previously empty cubicles, a team photographer, a few social media interns from the local college, and even an in-house designer who handles game day poster designs.

Until precisely this moment, I didn't even know that a game day poster was a thing, let alone that there was someone who had the position to create them. According to the gentleman in charge of design, each poster commemorates a specific match by paying homage to our team while displaying some tongue-in-cheek humor towards the opposing team visiting our stadium.

Soccer culture, I'm quickly learning, is really freaking weird.

At 12:30 P.M., precisely as indicated on my welcome sheet, my father ushers us to a dining facility within the stadium. Here, he tells me, the team nutritionist works closely with chefs to create and prepare meals for the players and staff. There is a separate kitchen within the offices where most front office staff choose to dine, but this dining facility is open to all members of the organization–from interns to players to even Maxwell Bigsby himself.

Today, only a few others are present in the dining hall. I recognize a few people I was previously introduced to throughout the morning, though after the barrage of introductions, names escape me. As my father steps aside to receive a phone call, a petite blond woman I haven't yet been introduced to comes over to where I'm seated, plopping herself across the table from me without asking.

"It isn't every day that Mr. Bigsby is here in the office. You must be someone extremely important to warrant such a personal welcome. What's your position for the team?"

I give her a shy grin, knowing that telling people I am the owner's daughter could potentially put a target on my back. Gesturing to my athletic pants and polo, I simply say, "I'm the new conditioning coach."

"Wait, I read a memo about you. Aren't you Bigsby's daughter? No offense, but you look nothing alike."

Well, she is certainly blunt and to the point.

"Yes, I'm Elle. And he is my adoptive father."

She nods as if my response makes all the sense in the world. "Well, I'm Ophelia. I work up top with the marketing team, but I'm sure we'll cross paths. Have you met the team yet? Man, those boys are going to eat you alive."

I don't ask what she means by that as she continues to talk. "I always like to come down here to eat when I can. You never know who you will run into. The players tend to stick to a tight group, but the eye candy is hard to pass up."

I tell her I haven't and continue to make small talk with her, glancing to where my father is still on his phone call.

"So, I guess soccer is kind of in your blood, isn't it?"

Shrugging, I let out a sigh. "Honestly, this is the first time I've ever been here, let alone had something to do with a soccer team. My goal is to work in the NFL, but I took this position for a year as a way to get my feet wet within the professional sports world. Cross my heart, I'm not getting any special treatment from him."

Ophelia puts her hand over mine. "Girl, it wouldn't bother me if you did. But anyways, I've got to run. I hope we get to see each other again soon."

As she makes to move, she turns back, glancing over her shoulder. "Hey, Elle, whatever you do, don't go falling in love with any of the players. Take it from experience, they're *nothing* but trouble."

With that, she winks before vanishing from the room, leaving me alone with my plate of expertly grilled chicken and sautéed asparagus.

After my father rejoins me and we finish our lunch, we head to the locker room. From what he tells me, the team will be arriving shortly. I follow Dad into an office tucked into the side of the large room. It surprises me how much it reminds me of our physical education teacher's office in high school. Like a fishbowl to the outside world, it is made of glass and decorated inside with numerous pictures of men shaking hands and holding trophies. There are two tall bookcases along the one wall not partitioned by glass, and they are stuffed full of binders with labels denoting their use.

I turn as an older gentleman enters the room, holding out his hand to clasp my father's in his. "Maxwell, great to see you." The gentleman turns a scrutinizing gaze on me. "You must be Eleanor?"

"Yes, please, call me Elle."

"Elle," He says my name matter-of-factly, as if he's stating the letter of the alphabet. "I can't say I am pleased with this move, and I have expressed as much to your father. But he assures me you will be a valuable asset to our team as our conditioning coach."

"Sir," I start to speak, but he interrupts me.

"James, please. Or Coach, if you prefer."

I take a deep breath. "Coach, I know my father putting me in this position is extremely unorthodox compared to how hiring practices are usually handled. I also know that I not only met but exceeded all expectations set forth of me while I was completing my studies. I have trained extensively to work along-side athletes and can assure you that my hard work and dedica-tion make me the perfect fit for this position, not my last name."

A curt nod is all he rewards me with.

I glance at the smartwatch on my wrist, noting we have a few minutes before I am set to meet the rest of the coaches and team. Excusing myself, I exit the locker room, finding a gender-inclusive restroom, before locking myself in the single stall and plopping myself onto the toilet seat without removing my pants.

My head falls into my hands as I take several long breaths.

In through the nose.

Hold for three.

Out through the mouth.

Repeat.

You can do this, Elle. It's only one year, and then you can take your talent to the NFL. You. Can. Do. This.

I give myself a few more minutes, silently hyping myself up. I splash a bit of cool water on my face and pat it dry, hoping the few tears that managed to squeeze out of my usually clogged tear ducts haven't left any marks. Pulling my phone from my pocket, I open up a countdown app I like to use to count the days until special events and add a new event to the list:

Days Till My Last Day At San Diego Sol: 365.

Returning to the locker room, I glance around at the bodies starting to fill the space and quickly notice the difference between these athletes and the American football players I've idolized much of my life. Where football players are big and meaty, these men are lean and uber-toned. As they remove street clothes and slip training shirts over their bodies, I can't help but take in their sinewy forms.

Corded muscular men strut around, drinking from water bottles, tossing snacks in their mouths, and joking with one another all while I stand by and silently watch as if I'm invisible.

My mind wanders as much as my eyes do, and not for the first time since Friday night, I'm reminded of the gorgeous mystery man I met at City Syn.

Jay.

My sister and a few of our mutual friends insisted on going to the posh nightclub to celebrate my new position; although, to me, it felt more like I was being given my last meal before being led to slaughter. Everyone in my family and all my friends were excited for me to start this chapter of my life, I just couldn't get on board with the same enthusiasm. I knew I needed experience to get my foot in the door with a professional football team; I just never pictured myself working for my dad's soccer team as the way to gain that experience.

Begrudgingly, I had allowed my group of closest friends to take me out to celebrate, and I even loosened up a bit on the dance floor. It felt freeing to throw my hands over my head, dancing along to the undulating beat of the music. I truly let go of whatever self-consciousness I may have had and allowed myself to just be in the moment.

Which, consequently, was how I found myself in a stranger's bed.

Well, technically, against a stranger's floor-to-ceiling windows overlooking the ocean, and then again over the arm of the aforementioned stranger's cushy armchair.

It was absolutely worth losing my debit card.

I had never allowed myself to be so free with a man before. Never truly allowed myself to reach deep down into my dirty girl psyche and ask for what I wanted. I was bold with Jay, and maybe it was because we didn't have any false pretenses of where the night would lead. It was one night.

One *glorious* night.

A male clearing his throat pulls me back to the present, and I feel my cheeks heat as I wonder how long I was standing there in a sexy, memory-induced haze.

I turn my head to meet my father's stare and quickly scurry back into the coach's office before stammering out my apology. "I...I'm sorry about that. I was just overwhelmed thinking of how grateful I am to share this opportunity with you."

Surely, both Coach and my dad can see right through my bullshit. But that's my story, and I'm sticking with it.

My dad walks back into the locker room, leaving the fishbowl office behind, where he shakes hands with several of the men and makes small talk with them about their families, the upcoming season, and what teams they are most looking forward to playing over the next several months. As Coach and I join them in the open space of the locker room, he speaks up, bringing all the eyes in the room to us.

"I see we are missing two members of the team, but let's begin." His voice is loud and commanding, and without ever seeing him on the soccer field, it's easy to see why he is a respected coach among the players. "It's great to see so many returning faces this season along with a few new players I have had the pleasure of meeting during the transfer window. You all either already know our staff well or have met them previously, but today, I have the pleasure," I don't miss the way he says the word, as if it's almost painful for him to say it, "of introducing you to Elle Bigsby. She will be joining us as our conditioning coach this season, and I expect you to give her just as much respect as you give me. Which, all things considered, isn't really much at all, is it?"

Several chuckles echo through the locker room.

"Alright, team, head for the pitch, and we'll be behind you in a few."

The men, sans Coach and my father, exit the room. When it is once again the three of us in the room, my father leans in, shaking Coach's hand. "I know she can hold her own but keep an eye on her."

Coach says nothing in return before walking back into his office, sitting at his desk as he goes through a stack of papers.

My father gives me a gentle squeeze on the shoulder before leaving the locker room to return to his cushy executive office.

Standing alone in the locker room, I already feel defeated. It's abundantly clear that Coach sees this as nothing more than my father pulling his weight to get his darling daughter a spot right out of college.

Well, little does he know that I want this.

No, I *need* this.

I'm willing to do the grunt work, to put in long hours to succeed, because if I can show Coach that I have what it takes, then I can prove to any NFL team out there that I can succeed with them, too.

Caught somewhere in my own mind, I don't hear the laughter trailing into the locker room from the hallway. My eyes are focused on the team bulletin board, a mishmash of information about the team, practices, and more written in a variety of languages. English, Spanish, and what looks to be Portuguese cover the board, and as I'm studying the information overload presented against the backdrop of cork, a gentle tap on the shoulder causes me to shoot up no less than six feet in the air before I plummet back to Earth, nearly falling on my ass in the process.

Before I fully crash down to the floor of the locker room, a pair of arms snake around my middle, catching me. A broad chest presses against my back, and my nose is drawn to the welcoming and somewhat familiar aroma of crisp cedarwood and warm vanilla.

A second person walks past me, entering Coach's office and taking a seat without a word to me.

Only then do I realize the mystery person's arms are still looped around my waist.

"I'm…I'm so sorry."

The voice behind me speaks as the arms simultaneously unwrap from my mid-section, and while my body misses the warmth of those hands and the strength of that broad chest against my back, my skin pricks at the voice speaking low and close to my ear. "Hello, again, Elle."

I gasp as I turn around, staring into the light blue eyes of my one-night-stand.

Jay.

A devious and cocky smirk spreads across his face as he reaches into his pocket, procuring something small. Gently placing my lost debit card into the palm of my hand, his grin turns dark, and his eyes flash with an emotion I can't read.

Jay turns to walk to Coach's fishbowl, looking back over his shoulder. "Or should I say…Eleanor."

He slams the door behind him, shutting me off from the rest of the locker room and leaving me alone, much like I did to him when I left his mansion when he ran to the bathroom to clean up after our night of mind-blowing sex.

I pull my phone from my pocket, tapping open the count-down app. Looking at the screen, I see the days haven't moved. Staring back at me, it still reads: *Days Till My Last Day At San Diego Sol: 365.*

SAN DIEGO SOL DECLINE TO COMMENT ON JENSEN WEST PHOTO SCANDAL.

Soccer Daily Online: For Immediate Release

Sol's star striker is amongst the latest celebrities to have photos sold to the media.

San Diego, CA, January 19- Jensen West, everybody's favorite bad boy soccer star, finds himself thrust into the media again, this time after a very public relationship gone wrong. Well known for his proficiency on the soccer field, he has recently become equally as well known for his proficiency below the belt.

Both San Diego Sol owner Maxwell Bigsby and Jensen West have declined to comment on the ongoing issue.

END RELEASE

The second the door fully closes behind us, he lays into me. Sure, Cole is standing right next to me, but all his ire is directed at me.

"Christ, West!" His voice is loud, bouncing off the walls of his glass office. "It's the first damn day of pre-season, and you're already showing up late! I know last season was rough for you, but you really need to step it up and show that you want to be a part of this team."

I don't say anything–simply let him tear into me.

"Unless. . .this is your way of showing you don't value being part of this club. Is that what you're trying to show me?"

Honestly, I'm not really sure how I feel about anything anymore, especially when it comes to my career.

I thought I had more time when I was playing in the Premier League, thought I had more time playing overall before words like "forced retirement" and "advanced athletic age" started circulating next to my name, more time before I started having to look at coaching and commentating as opposed to running on the pitch, the turf under me as my feet desperately itched to connect with the ball before sending it to the back of the net.

Coach stares back at me, dark brown eyes boring into my soul as he waits for an answer.

"I promise you that I value being part of this club, Coach. I won't be late again."

Damnit, here I am, in my thirties, and it still feels like I'm back in primary school, being scolded in the principal's office after convincing a bunch of my mates to help me fill the librarian's tiny office to the brim with ping pong balls.

Actually, that was pretty fucking hilarious.

Wonder how pissed Coach would get if we did the same to him?

Quickly, I shake that idea from my head.

Coach stalks behind his desk, opening a drawer before pulling a magazine from within. He shoves it toward me, wanting to get his hands off of the glossy cover as quickly as possible.

"Seriously, West." His voice is lower now, almost ominous. "Get your shit together before the season starts, or you won't be seeing playing minutes."

Opening the door, he rejoins Elle, leaving me and Cole alone in his office.

Slowly, I peel the magazine away from my chest and look at the cover. It comes into Cole's view at the same time as it does mine, and my idiot best friend roars with laughter as I groan.

A naked version of myself graces the bright yellow cover of the magazine with nothing but a very strategically placed football covering my goods. I look slightly shocked in the picture, mouth in a small o-shape as I gaze straight ahead.

And that's for good reason.

"Mother fucking Cecilia."

I'm clenching my teeth so tightly that it is a surprise my molars don't crack from impact, and I swear I can actually feel the blood boiling as it courses through my veins.

Her nasally voice runs through my head. *"Oh, come on, Jensen! You know I would never show these to anyone. You know how much it turns me on to be able to see all of you when you're traveling, to feel like I'm close to you."*

Red clouds my field of vision as I read the banner across the top of the magazine as well as the article headline on the cover.

Man of the Month Jensen West Bares It All!

Jensen West: What Drives Him Wild!?

Six months.

I wasted six months of my life on Cecilia Van Hutchinson—the social media influencer turned model turned wannabe pop star. She was known around the world for slinging skin-care products made with the secretions of jellyfish or some other bizarre shit like that.

I told her I wanted to keep it casual, but she fell fast and hard. And while I was off playing football and trying to clean up my image, she was demanding more and more of my time until I couldn't take it anymore. In hindsight, taking her to a fancy restaurant to break things off probably wasn't my brightest idea, but at the time, I was just praying that taking her into public to go our separate ways would keep her from having a meltdown of epic proportions.

Instead, she was under the assumption that I was taking her out for a night on the town to propose. When I told her over dessert that I thought it was best if we didn't see each other anymore, she threw an entire baked Alaska at me while it was still on fire before storming from the restaurant in tears, all the while screaming that I would regret my decision to end our relationship.

Like I said—hindsight.

Making the mistake of looking at the magazine again, the rage fully returns to my body. I whip the magazine across the office, sending a picture crashing to the ground as I yell into the small space.

"Jay!" Cole's deep voice along with his hand on my shoulder

pulls me from my rage. "Keep it together, mate. You're off your trolley."

Fuck, he's right.

I take a few deep breaths and look around the office before going in search of a dustpan to clean up my mess.

Another twenty minutes pass before I finally show my face to the rest of the team.

Picking up a rogue ball tumbling near me, I walk toward Cole and several of the other guys who are already in the middle of the first-day fitness tests that are common amongst athletes. Pausing a few steps short, something catches my attention from the corner of my eye.

Elle is standing off to the side of the pitch, arms stretched above her body as she gathers her fiery red curls into a heap on top of her head. Missing several strands, a few loose tendrils tumble down around her face, and as my eyes follow those strands of hair, I find myself captivated by the slope of her beautiful neck, now unobstructed by her wild curls.

She's listening as several of the team's various coaches chat, nodding along enthusiastically. To the casual observer, you would think she is enjoying the conversation.

But I'm not a casual observer.

Elle takes her hair out of its pile, letting curls cascade down around her face before immediately gathering the strands in her fingers, securing them on top of her head again. Fidgeting with the strands that have once again escaped her attempt to gather them, she rocks back and forth on her feet–as if she's had one too many drinks–while choosing to dart her eyes from one focal point within the stadium to the next, never holding eye contact with any of her fellow coaches.

Eleanor Bigsby is unsure of herself.

But why?

Growing up on the dodgy outskirts of London left a lot to be desired for me. My childhood consisted of second-hand clothes, often with holes, that came to me via my older brother. My shoes were either too small or too big, but never just quite right. I was lucky if I got a haircut more than twice a year, the months in between managed by my mum and a rusty pair of kitchen shears. When we weren't going hungry, we subsided on cheap meals of rice or peanut butter sandwiches.

Don't get me wrong; my parents tried to keep us fed and clothed, but with two boys and three girls–all within four years of one another–some corners just had to be cut. My brother and sister– twins–were two years older than I was. I followed along next before another surprise set of twins–this time two baby girls– completed our family.

After my younger sisters were born, Mum left her job as a primary school teacher to stay home with us, leaving my dad's income as our sole earnings. I wanted desperately to do normal things like every other kid my age–after school sports, day trips, going out with friends on the weekends–but finances always held me and my siblings back.

Above all else though, I wanted to play football. I envied the posh kids I saw running on the pitch after school, shiny new boots on their feet as they chased the ball. I envied my mates who got to travel by bus to other towns and cities to play against other teams, envied the boys I saw going with their fathers to actually *see* famous teams like Liverpool, who had existed within the same space since the late 1800s.

And though I was just a lad at the time, I knew that I somehow *had* to make it happen.

So, I did.

Doing odd chores for my neighbors–everything from yard work to washing cars–I saved up enough to buy my first ball. I practiced every spare minute of my day, going as far as to sneak off before school to run drills I had made up after watching the other kids play.

Early one morning, I snuck off to an abandoned field by my

house. It was overgrown and only had a net at one end of the pitch. But it was my happy place. I had been weaving between imaginary cones, practicing my speed, when a sandy-haired boy walked up to me alongside an older gentleman that looked just like him, only thirty years or so older.

Cole, it had turned out, had seen me practicing on my own almost every day as he walked to school, and even at the young age of ten, thought he saw something special in me. His father, the gentleman with him that day, worked for an academy with a dedication to the sport, and at Cole's insistent nagging, agreed to accompany his son to see if his intuition was right.

The next morning, the pair returned to the field where I was already deep in my solitary practice. They brought along small cones and additional balls, goalkeeper gloves, and a speed ladder. But what I'll never forget most, was on that day, they also brought along what would become my very first pair of boots. Yes, they were hand-me-downs, and yes, they were scuffed and scratched, but when I slid my feet into those boots, they fit.

Not too small.

Not too big.

I was like the Goldilocks of the fucking football pitch, and hand to God, the minute those magical shoes were affixed to my feet, my life changed.

After several days where Cole and his father would meet me each morning, they asked if they could meet my parents, and when we arrived back at mine, Cole's father explained who he was, as well as the situation that brought us together.

What felt like hundreds of conversations and millions of pages of paperwork later, I was a proud scholarship recipient and was afforded the opportunity to train alongside Cole at the prestigious school his father worked for.

So, as I stood here now, watching Eleanor Bigsby fidget with anything her fingers could grasp, I knew that what looked like a woman casually observing her new co-workers was actually her being nervous.

Interesting.

While my mind continually drifts, I'm finally able to pull my head out of my own ass long enough to focus on practice. We run through drills, practice taking shots on goal, break down into smaller teams to run through specialized training based on our positions, then finish with some stretching before Coach blows his whistle, motioning us all toward the plush chairs the team sits in during matches.

Despite the air around us being cool, practice has left me covered in sweat, and as I take a seat on the grass, I down an entire bottle of water before pulling my shirt over my head, dumping a second bottle over myself.

I don't miss the way Eleanor glances at me, watching as the water rivulets travel over my body before soaking into the waistband of my shorts.

Wonder if she's looking at those water droplets and thinking back to the slick sheen of sweat that coated both our bodies just days ago?

Well, now I sure as hell am.

Still, something about the woman doesn't rub me the right way. Did she *really* not know who I was when we met on Friday? Hell, her dad owns the fucking team; certainly, she has spent time around the sport. What has her so on edge around the rest of the coaching staff, and why does she act like she's never even seen a soccer ball before?

I fully intend to get to the bottom of the mystery that is Eleanor Bigsby, but in the meantime, I'm going to enjoy making her squirm.

Uncapping a third bottle of water, I bring it to my lips, letting the cold liquid course down my throat, cooling me from the inside out. As I continue to drink, I seek out her eyes with my own, holding their focus for several seconds, knowing the attention is surely making her more uncomfortable than she has already shown to be all practice.

And then, I wink.

Her cheeks rapidly redden as her eyes fly away from mine. Hands flying through her hair, she allows the curls to tumble as if creating a curtain to shield herself away from my eyes.

She's saved by the proverbial bell as Coach takes center stage, quieting the chatter that has started around us.

"Over the next few days, each of you will be meeting individually with Elle. As you all know, she will be working closely with Coach Terry to make sure you are all in top fitness for game day. She will be evaluating you, looking for areas of improvement. You looked good out there today, boys, but good doesn't cut it in this league. I sure as hell don't want a repeat of last season, and I know none of you who were with Sol last year want that either. Head in and change; you've got a half hour until we meet up for dinner."

Most teams in the MLS had their own traditions, some more serious and some downright bonkers. We were no different.

Each year on the first day of training, we would have a team dinner prepared by our staff–expertly crafted food designed to signify the start of a new season and ease us into the transition of often grueling practices. Yes, most of us stuck to pretty strict nutrition and workout regimens even during the off-season, but it wasn't uncommon to put on a few extra pounds during those months.

That was our more serious tradition.

The downright bonkers tradition, now *that* was my favorite.

I have absolutely no idea when it first happened–maybe our second season in the league. We had a teammate at the time who had a secret talent for painting and when the team found out, a few of the lads challenged him to a paint-off. They each chose a player from the team, attempted to paint a portrait of the chosen player, and shared the results. That night, I nearly pissed myself laughing as tears rolled down my cheeks. The results were downright heinous, and of course, even more of the team wanted to try their hand at the challenge.

Now, on our first night of practice, it has become a tradition for us to draw names from a cap and paint the player we randomly choose.

For the record, not one of us since that first teammate has an artistic bone in our bodies. Hell, give me a coloring book, and I can barely stay in the damn lines.

Regardless, it's still a tradition I look forward to each year.

Our team, including the coaching staff, heads into a large conference room where tables have been topped with easels, canvases, paints, and brushes. Finding a spot, I get down to the business of utterly butchering a portrait of our goalkeeper, Schmidt.

Classic rock is pumping through the room, but you can barely hear it over the sounds of laughter coming from my team-mates and the coaching staff.

My stomach already hurts from laughing as I swirl colors together and slap them on canvas.

Scanning the room, my eyes find Eleanor. Her head is thrown back as she laughs at something one of the guys said, and as she laughs, the long column of her neck is exposed.

I want to lick up that long neck.

To nip and bite at it as she writhes beneath me.

Down, boy.

Most everyone is finishing up, wiping their hands of misplaced paint while cackling at their own creations.

Coach gives a ten-minute warning to the team and off to the side, Eleanor sneaks out of the room.

I follow, ready to get some answers.

As I enter the hall, the door to the bathroom closes, and before she has time to lock the single-person stall, I push in behind her.

Wild eyes spin around, locking on my own.

"What the fuck?"

Closing in on her space, I walk backward until she is against the wall, my hips nearly pushing against hers. "Tell me the truth, Eleanor. Did you know who I was?"

Those same bottle-green, wild eyes go wide. "What? No!"

I cage her in, one hand on each side of her head, pressed into the cold concrete of the wall as I tower over her. "So, you're saying it's a complete coincidence that I met you this weekend, fucked the absolute life out of you, and then walk into work today to find you standing in the locker room? You understand how I find that *very* hard to believe?"

Her nostrils flare in what I can only assume is rage. "If I recall correctly, *Jay*," she says my name with so much venom that it drips from her tongue, "you were the one who came on to me." A short, pink-painted nail comes to land on my chest. "You were the one who approached *me*, who asked *me* to dance, who asked *me* to come home with you. How in the hell would I have known who *you* are?"

I scoff incredulously, "Because I'm Jensen fucking West!"

She laughs loudly, and in the small space, the echo bouncing off the walls hurts my eardrums. "Well, Jensen *fucking* West, not everybody cares about fucking soccer. Now, get the hell out of the bathroom so I can pee in peace!"

"If you don't care about *soccer*," I imitate her voice as I say the words, "what are you doing here?"

This time, both of her palms connect with my chest as she tries to push me away. "That doesn't concern you!"

Leaning down to speak directly into her ear, I snarl out my response. "This team and its success are my top concern because when this team succeeds, I succeed. So yes, it *does* concern me, Eleanor. As long as you are here, you are my concern, too."

I hear the sound and feel my face fly to the side before it registers that her open palm has just connected with my cheek.

She. Slapped. Me.

And honestly, it kind of hurt.

But I'll be damned if I let her know that.

Instead, I push back from the wall, a low chuckle rumbling from deep within coming from my mouth. "Damn, Princess, if I would have known you were that feisty, I would have given it to you even rougher on Friday."

Eleanor is still against the wall when I reach the door, chest heaving as she breathes. I don't wait to find out if it is from anger or lust, but I'm pretty sure it is the former of the two emotions. Slipping out of the door while keeping my eyes on her, I hear the lock as it clicks behind me and turn around, only to walk into my best friend.

Cole smirks. "Already trying to fuck the babysitter?"

I'm silently seething, knowing that Eleanor being here every day will surely be the bane of my existence. I lean next to Cole, propping myself on the brick wall of the hallway. "That babysitter is the woman I took home from the club on Friday."

A rumble of laughter bubbles up through him. "Oh, this is too good, Jay. Too fucking good. Day one and you're already fucking the boss's daughter!"

"Not fucking! Fucked–as in once. It will not be happening again."

"Yeah, right." Cole snorts when he laughs again.

The door to the bathroom opens, and Eleanor slinks out. When our eyes connect, she quickly looks away.

"Hey, Red," Cole calls, grabbing her attention. "Looking forward to working with you. Maybe we can throw some yoga into our work. You know, strengthen my core a bit more, make me a bit more flexible."

The asshole pulls his shirt up, running his opposite hand over his toned stomach as he shoots her a wink. Eleanor's cheeks flame in response, turning almost the same color as her hair. She gives him an infinitesimal nod, shoots one last glare in my direction, and walks back into the conference room.

"The fuck was that, Cole?" I spit the words out through clenched teeth.

"I mean, she's a little chubby for my taste, but there is no denying there is something kind of hot about her. If you're not going after her, I might as well shoot my shot. Unless you want to share, it wouldn't be the first time we've done that. Remember that night in Ibiza with…"

I shove him before he can finish, my anger reaching an almost nuclear level. "She's off limits, man. I'm not touching her again, you're not touching her, and no one else on this team will touch her. Off. Fucking. Limits."

He rubs at his arm where I shoved him, acting dramatic as ever.

Turning to walk back to the conference room, he calls out after me, still laughing, "We'll see, Jay. We'll see."

Never before in my life have I hated Cole.

Until now.

PRESEASON GAMES TO BEGIN THIS WEEK.

Soccer Daily Online: For Immediate Release

San Diego Sol is scheduled to take on several west coast rivals during their preseason matchups.

San Diego, CA, February 13- While the full season will see the team facing matchups across the country, many of the team's preseason matchups will be against other California teams vying for the top spot as Football King of the West.

Coach James Calder is quoted as saying, "While we thoroughly enjoy playing all the teams in our league, there is something uniquely special about playing another team from the same state. The energy and atmosphere the supporters bring to the game cannot be beat, even during a preseason match."

END RELEASE

IT'S BEEN ALMOST a month of daily practice, almost a month of pretending that I know what I'm doing when it comes to conditioning a soccer team, and almost a month of trying to avoid Jensen West.

It wasn't easy at first.

Actually, it still isn't.

The first day, I was mortified when Coach asked me to meet him and the rest of the team on the field for practice. I stood around for ten minutes, waiting for the players and coaches to turn up, but they never did. Coach Terry, the fitness coach I work in tandem with, found me on the field and delicately explained to me that our team practices are on a different field than where they actually play games. Embarrassedly walking alongside him, we made our way to an open expanse of greenery behind the stadium, to a field slightly smaller than the one I had seen earlier in the day. Littered with different training apparatuses, balls, and water bottles, I found a place on the sideline and quietly watched the activities flurrying around me.

At least now, I can find my way to the training facility without a chaperone.

One thing that hasn't changed is the absolute hate that flows daily between me and Jensen. After our third day of practice, I walked to the parking garage to find my car entirely covered in sticky notes–windows and all. It took me almost a half hour to remove enough of them from the windows to the point it was safe enough to drive home to my apartment. All the way, little pieces of paper were floating behind me, causing other commuters to either honk at me, flip me the bird, or laugh as they passed.

It may have been childish of me, but I retaliated by swapping his protein powder that he kept in his locker with baking flour the next day.

About a week later, I legitimately peed my pants a little when I went to toss something in the industrial-sized washing machine on site, only to be startled when Jensen jumped out wearing a Scream mask and holding a fake knife. Thank God for the change of clothes I keep in my locker.

Of course, I wasn't going to let him skate on that prank, and a few days after he pulled his stunt, I snuck into the room where all the player's gear is stored and hid all of his left soccer cleats.

The dude *flipped*–pulled me into a small conference room and yelled at me, saying that I could do whatever I wanted, but if I touched his boots–as he calls them–that he would make sure my life was hell.

As if he didn't already do that every damn day.

Despite these stupid games with Jensen that I keep finding myself up against, there has been a lot of good over the last month, too. The best part of each day has been lunch in the team-appointed kitchen. Today, like most other days, I hear Ophelia before she comes to sit down at the small two-top table I'm currently sitting at along a beige wall.

Her white-blond hair hangs down in an even curtain around her face, a stark difference to my own wild, red curls. Wearing a slim pencil skirt and ruffled, sleeveless top along with a pair of heels, we're quite the study in contrast as I sit across from her in a team polo, joggers, and an old pair of tennis shoes.

"Derek Morgan or Dr. Spencer Reid?"

I look at her quizzically, although I'm slowly learning to anticipate the crazy questions she brings to our almost daily lunch.

Ophelia picks up her fork, stabbing a piece of broccoli and popping it into her mouth before continuing, "If you were kidnapped and being held hostage and you could only have Derek Morgan or Dr. Spencer Reid as your rescuer, which one would you choose? I mean, I assume you've seen the television masterpiece that is *Criminal Minds*?"

I laugh, finishing my own bite of food with a swallow while contemplating the two choices. "Oh, yeah, I've streamed each season several times. And...probably Derek Morgan. Don't get me wrong; they're both extremely capable men, but he's the kind of man who makes you feel safe."

She giggles. "Is it that he is an extremely capable man, or is it that whole alpha *baby girl* vibe he gives off?"

Pausing to think for a second, she starts again before I can interject. "Oh, my God, Elle, you have a praise kink, don't you? You just *know* he'd wrap you in those big, strong arms before whisking you off to his bedroom, telling you the entire time that you were so brave, so strong, such a good girl."

Ophelia coos the words, and I can't help but start laughing again. "You really are kinda crazy, you know that?"

"Yeah, but you kinda like me, so it all works out. Plus, I don't hear you denying it. You're totally a freak in the sheets, aren't you?"

Quickly, she has turned into a real friend at work, and it's true; I do enjoy having her in my life just as much as I do enjoy being praised in the bedroom. While she works for the marketing team, her knowledge of the sport far surpasses mine, and I have been able to rely on her whenever I've had a question that I was too embarrassed to bring to my fellow coaches.

"What about you?" I ask, bringing the last bite of lunch to

my mouth while ignoring her last question regarding my bedroom practices.

"Simple. I'd take both."

"You said I could only choose one to save me?"

"That's the beauty of it, Elle. I ask the questions, so I make the rules. And if I want Derek Morgan *and* Dr. Spencer Reid in my rescue fantasy, then dammit, I'm going to have them both."

"Funnily enough, Ophelia, I feel like you're no longer talking about a fantasy where they rescue you."

She leans in close to me, glancing around to assure no one else can overhear our conversation. "You're right. And in this fantasy, they're totally crossing swords."

I can feel my eyes bulge out of their sockets as I stare at my friend, mouth agape, before bursting out in laughter that has me wiping the corner of my eyes with my napkin.

Behind us, the door opens, and the sounds of deep voices chattering fill the space around us. Noticeably, Ophelia straightens her posture a bit, tucking one ankle behind the other in an almost princess-like move as she sweeps her hair behind her shoulders. Several of the players pass us on the way to retrieve their food, nodding or exchanging polite pleasantries with us on their way. Once they are out of earshot, my friend turns back to me, hearts floating in her crystal-blue eyes. "I still can't believe you get to be around those absolutely delicious men all day."

The door opens again, Jensen and his closest cohort, Cole, entering the room. While most of the team appears to get along well, it's not lost on me that Jensen and Cole seem to be some-what of the team outliers. They stick near one another both on the field and off, and when one is seen, it can be expected that the other isn't far behind. From the bits and pieces of conversation I've managed to overhear over the last few weeks, it sounds like they have history, playing on many of the same teams together over the years.

A gentle wrapping on the table distracts me from my thoughts, and I turn my face to see Cole's knuckles connect with the table once again. "Hey, Elle, looking forward to our session this afternoon. Hoping we can open up my hip flexors with some gentle stretching before I hop on the massage table later today. Unless you think you could help me out with that, too?"

I don't get to respond before Jensen pushes his friend, growling as he moves him towards the chef's daily creation. He locks eyes with me, only long enough to glare at me, before following in his friend's footsteps.

"What the actual fuck was that?"

Glancing at Ophelia, I shake my head. "He's just trying to get under Jensen's skin."

She looks at me skeptically, her brow furrowing. "And *why* would he be doing that? Do you have a thing for him?"

Sighing defeatedly, I delve into the story, a wide-eyed Ophelia staring at me in awe the entire time. I tell her about the first night we met at City Syn, about the mind-blowing sex, sneaking out of his house in the middle of the night, and him returning my debit card on the first day of training. I recall his icy behavior in the bathroom stall and how he has gone out of his way to ignore me, only breaking long enough to shoot me the occasional daggers from across a room or the training field or to play some childish prank on me that I, of course, *have* to reciprocate.

I finish what should surely stand as a cautionary tale to anyone wanting to get involved with a professional athlete and take my friend's hands earnestly across the table. "Please, Ophelia, this does *not* leave this table. The only person who knows about this outside the two of us is my sister and Jensen."

"Naturally, that means Cole knows, too."

I nod, knowing she is right.

One of the best parts of my job is taking a group of grown and toned adults and working them until they are on their knees, begging for forgiveness.

Cole may have been joking about stretching out his hip flexors earlier, but to anyone who has studied conditioning and the body, it's apparent that this group of professional athletes has never tried yoga a day in their lives. I know Coach James and Coach Terry have the best interest of their team in mind, but the men, both significantly older than myself, are inherently old school when it comes to training.

Much of my first week at Sol was spent observing. Aside from meeting with each player one-on-one to talk about their personal goals, I was a silent bystander, letting the more tenured coaching staff take the reins. But as I slowly became more comfortable with the coaching staff and my players, I began to actively seek out ways to improve the team. And as I started to provide my thoughts, especially to Coach Terry, more of my input was asked for.

Which leads me to my current situation.

Me, in front of over a dozen grown men, walking them through poses designed to not only relax their bodies but strengthen them as well.

"Today is strictly being used as a way for me to gauge your flexibility and level of comfort with some exercises you may not be familiar with. Over the next few weeks, I'll be customizing a specialized program for each of you that will build upon your strengths and focus on improving your weaknesses."

There is grunting in response—which coming from this group of men is strangely attractive—sweating, more than a few curse words being muttered out loud, and I'm fairly certain more than one of these men has passed gas while trying to blame it on their neighbor.

Noticeably missing from the group?

The one and only Jensen West.

He's like my very own Lost Boy, always off on his own while the rest of the team puts forth the effort to improve. I think back to my first day of training, when he caged me in the bathroom.

"This team and its success are my top concern because when this team succeeds, I succeed."

For a man who is overly concerned with success, he sure as hell has a funny way of showing it.

"Hey, Coach Elle!" I scan the room, finding our goalkeeper, Jonathan Schmidt, twisted into a human pretzel on the soft yoga mat allocated to him. "How am I doing?"

Walking over to the large man, I drop to the ground, helping him to position his right knee between his hands that are outstretched in front of him. Of all the men on the team, he has been among the friendliest to me since my arrival, going out of his way to greet me each day and even pulling up a chair once or twice to sit in on a friendly lunch with Ophelia and myself. There is absolutely nothing sexual between us, but it's nice to have one of the guys on my side.

Looking around, a small sense of pride creeps up as I watch the team in various states of the Pigeon Pose I have them seated in. "This position is a deep hip opening pose and will help to stretch your quadriceps, too. Cole, pay special attention to this one; it's also fantastic for your hip flexors.

If you're feeling confident in your pose, you can transform into Sleeping Pigeon by bending slightly, being sure to support your upper body with your forearms. If that still feels easy to you, try to bring yourself completely flush to the floor."

I return to the front of the group, demonstrating each of the steps. Several of the guys attempt the hardest iteration of the pose and someone's voice, I'm not sure which man it came from, chirps up. "Christ, I thought this shit was gonna be easy, but I have sweat dripping down my ass crack."

Laughter rolls around the room, which I am not excluded from.

"Try to hold each pose for six to eight deep breaths. My favorite part of yoga is that, while it helps to stretch out your body and can elongate your muscles, it's also a fantastic way to relieve stress and tension. And I'm sure with the workload and preparation you each take on before games that this is something that could benefit your brains just as much as your forms."

We walk through several other poses that have additional benefits for soccer players–Downward Dog, Squatting Crow, and Bridge Pose–and all the while, I demonstrate the fluid motions before walking the room, helping the men tuck themselves into proper form.

As we are on the last circuit of our routine, the hair on the back of my neck stands on edge, and I suddenly feel like the air has been sucked from the room. Completing an advanced demonstration of Downward Dog into a Transverse Twist, I turn my head and lock eyes with Jensen.

Quickly, I bring myself up while pulling down on my polo that had slightly ridden up my stomach. I can't help the sarcasm as I speak. "Mr. West, how nice of you to join us."

Addressing the rest of the room, I instruct the men to cool down with a few simple breathing techniques before dismissing them to the locker room, all the while Jensen stands statue still, observing the rest of his teammates.

Several long minutes pass, the team rolling up yoga mats and storing them alongside a wall before they slowly file out of the room. One by one they leave, thanking me for the time, commenting on their favorite positions, and playfully bantering with me about the workout.

Cole is the last to leave, shooting me a wink and clapping Jensen on the shoulder before exiting the room, calling after himself with a, "Can't wait to do it again, Red."

Jensen and I stand there, locked in an apparent battle of wills, neither one of us willing to concede by speaking first. Ultimately, I cave, throwing his words from the first day of practice back in his face. "For someone who claims they care about this team and its success, you have a fucked-up way of showing it. Do you even care about playing for Sol, or is this all just some sort of weird game to you?"

Making to leave the room, his large hand grips my wrist, stopping me in my tracks and almost searing into my skin. I simultaneously want to pull away from his grip and beg him to take me up against the nearest wall. "Don't fucking test me, Eleanor. You know nothing about me, nothing about my life, or what I go through every day. Stick to playing coach for Daddy's team, but stay the fuck out of my way. I'm sure you've been handed everything you ever wanted, this job included."

I shake from his vice grip, using all my strength to push him away from me. Seething, I refuse to let him see how much his words hurt, how the sting of them burrow deep into my soul where every insecurity I've ever had about being known as a Bigsby sits, just waiting to rear their ugly heads.

All my life, people have assumed that I have been able to get what I want because of my last name–due to who my father is and the company he keeps in high places.

But they're wrong.

It's why I've kept my circle of friends close and small, spending time with my sister and only a few of our mutual friends. It's why I've kept my head down, studying even harder than everyone else around me. It's why I've been pouring over *Soccer for Dummies* at night, watching old Sol games on the weekends, and reading everything I can get my hands on about conditioning for soccer players.

Because when I succeed, I want it to be on my own merit, not on the back of Maxwell Bigsby. I love my father, I truly do. But the success I'm looking for needs to come on my own.

I reach the door without Jensen's hands touching me again, a silent sigh of relief escaping from my now tense body. Before leaving, I turn back to him somewhere in a place between self-preservation and self-deprecation. Searching his blue eyes, I see nothing but hatred–toward me or something bigger, I'm not sure. But I am confident that it breaks my heart to have anyone hate me, even Jensen West.

I give him a sad smile, shrugging one shoulder up to my ear before dropping it defeatedly. "If it makes you feel any better, Jay, I don't want to be here anymore than you want me here. Let's just try to play nice. It will make the season go by a hell of a lot smoother for both of us, and then, you'll be rid of me for good."

I walk away.

TAKING TRAINING TO THE GREAT OUTDOORS.

Soccer Daily Online: For Immediate Release

San Diego Sol trades training grounds for famed San Diego landmark.

San Diego, CA, February 16- While soccer clubs around the country are preparing for their final stretch before the season's official start date, San Diego Sol looks to have taken a unique approach to training. The team, joined by members of their coaching staff, were spotted on the famed South Fortuna Steps, where they seemed to be enjoying a combination of training and sightseeing.

The team could not be reached for comment.

END RELEASE

Between training and preseason games, I am beat. While the guys don't say it, I can tell they're feeling it, too. Most of them are spending more time each day in ice baths or on the massage table, and the season hasn't even officially started yet. I, on the other hand, work with the guys throughout the day before returning to my apartment and sinking into a long, hot bubble bath almost nightly.

The tub in my apartment is tiny–one of those tubs where you can choose to have either your tits or your knees submerged, but never both at the same time. Still, the lavender bubble bath I drizzle into the water as it fills the tub helps to relax my sore muscles while calming my mind at the same time.

We're a few days away from traveling to Los Angeles for another scrimmage, but today, to break up the monotony of training, I have something fun planned for the team before we leave.

At least, it's going to be fun for me. The guys, on the other hand, might hate me for it.

It took some convincing on my part, but after several days of back and forth, Coach agreed that it would be good to get out of the training complex for a day before we really start with the grueling travel schedule the season brings. I had some ideas swirling in my head, but I kept coming back to one of my favorite things to do in San Diego.

The South Fortuna Steps are a San Diego staple and something I've done countless times with my family and friends over the years. At just about five miles, the trail is the smallest of the area's five peaks, but that doesn't make it any less challenging.

The bus full of men pulls into a gravel lot where Coach and I are already waiting, water bottles in hand. One by one, they step down from their transportation, both looking around at the scenery and eyeing me suspiciously.

Once they all gather around us, Coach speaks up. "I've given Coach Elle full reign over training today, and while I'm a little more traditional in my approach, I agree with her that this departure from our normal routine will benefit all of us, myself included. I've been carefully watching her with all of you over the last few weeks and will say she has greatly exceeded my expectations."

He gestures to me, stepping back to give me center stage. "I know many of you come from places around the world, and that you might not have time to explore San Diego in your limited down time. Today, I'm going to combine our daily training with a bit of sightseeing. Most of you run between seven to nine miles during a game, so a five-mile little hike should be a piece of cake, right?"

I hear a few grunts of affirmation, while others choose to nod in agreement.

"Who thinks they can be the first to complete the hike?" I ask the group.

Again, I get a few responses. A few others raise their hand.

Silly boys–always so eager to prove themselves.

"One last thing before we start, I wanted to give you a bit of history of the trail. While the full name of the area we're hiking is the South Fortuna Trail, what makes it unique is that there are over three hundred natural wooden stairs built into the side of the climb. Some people call it the *Stairway to Heaven,* but others simply call it Hell for the leg workout they get from running the steps."

Blank faces stare back at me.

"Stairs?" Jensen is the first to break the group's silence.

"Yup," I respond, popping the P for emphasis. "Most people can finish the trail in about three hours, but I think you guys can do better than that."

I toss a stopwatch at Coach Terry, who is staying behind to time the team before starting towards the trail. "You guys aren't going to get very far by standing there!" Taking a few more steps, I turn around to see that, with the exception of Coach, they're all still standing around looking dumbfounded. With one last attempt at motivation, I pull the ace out of my back pocket that I've been holding on to for exactly this moment. "Did I mention there is a prize for the winner?"

And with that, they start clamoring around, grabbing bottles of water before running ahead of me toward the climb.

Men–when in doubt, turn it into a game for them, and they'll eat up whatever you throw their way.

Staying toward the front of the pack for the first half of the hike, I'm on pace to hit my own personal record for the trail. It makes me proud to know that even though I might not look the part, my body is good to me, and I can keep up with some of the world's best athletes. The knowledge has a wide smile on my face as I chat casually with the guys.

Perhaps the biggest surprise of the day is watching Jensen and Cole as they compete with not only their teammates but with one another as well. Through playful banter, the two vie for top place, continually passing one another as they race toward the top of the summit.

Schmidt comes up from behind, breathing heavily. "I never knew you were a sadist, Coach."

Jensen calls from ahead, "Don't let her lie to you, Schmidtty. She may enjoy punishing us, but she's a masochist at her core."

I feel my cheeks flush as my mind flits back to the one night we shared–me on my knees in front of him as he came on my face and in my hair. Yeah, maybe I am a bit of a masochist, but I don't need the entire team knowing about my bedroom preferences.

"Fuck off, Jay!" I holler back, not caring that there are other hikers on the trail.

We haven't let up on the games we've been playing with one another almost relentlessly either. Last week, I walked into my small office to find everything in the entire room had been wrapped in aluminum foil. From my computer to my phone down to my office chair and picture frames on my desk. When I got everything unwrapped, the photos of my family and friends all had been replaced with pictures of Jeff Goldblum. Not that I minded that part–the man is a silver fox.

I retaliated by sneaking into the locker room before the team was done with training and taped all his personal items from his locker to the ceiling. Coming back in from training, he looked around for his phone and keys, accusing Cole of taking them before the laughter and upward-turned eyes of the other players caught his attention.

Coach calls from further down the trail, "Children, do I have to separate you?"

Through all our back and forth, Coach has been surprisingly cool, not asking us to stop or go easy on one another. I think he knows something happened between us in the past, but he's the type of guy who believes that some things are better left unknown.

Our group makes it to the top, some of the guys stopping to catch their breath under the guise of taking pictures of the view of San Diego below us, while others, myself included, continue on toward the awaiting team bus.

Beating us all back to the bus is our backup goalkeeper, a twenty-year-old from Venezuela. Coach Terry announces his official time before I present him with his prize, a two-night stay at a luxury spa in San Diego. I had to pull a few strings to get it, but having something to motivate the guys while coming through with a killer prize was totally worth it.

We all work through a few stretches to end the day before grabbing waters that have been kept cold in several coolers.

Leaning against my car while enjoying a bottle of cool water, Jensen makes his way over to me after joining the group, dumping a bottle of water over his head along the way. "I've got to give credit where credit is due, Eleanor. You held your own up there with us."

I give a little smile, not completely ready to let my guard down around him.

"You coming back to the stadium with the rest of the team?"

Shaking my head, I answer him, "Nope, family dinner tonight. I have to head home and get ready."

"Do you do that often–family dinners?" He looks at me intently, almost wistfully. I imagine it's hard for him to be away from his family, much like it is for all the athletes on the team.

Deciding to be honest instead of giving him a smart-ass remark like I normally would, I answer, "If by often, you mean about once every three years, then absolutely."

Okay, so maybe that answer was still a little sassy.

He gives me a smile–a genuine smile that stretches across his face. It's a smile that is guarded, one that I haven't seen since the night we first met.

Pushing away from the car, he tugs at a curl that had long ago escaped the confines of the hat I wore to block the sun from my face. "Well then, guess I'll see you when we head out to Los Angeles. See you later, red."

I climb into my car, preparing to drive away, but I pause to take one last look back at my team. I'm not surprised that my feelings about my team have started to shift over the last few weeks, but I am surprised to find Jensen still looking in my direction, a pensive look on his face.

Maybe he and I are making progress towards civility after all.

SAN DIEGO SOL TO TAKE ON LA GALAXY IN LAST PRESEASON MATCH.

Soccer Daily Online: For Immediate Release

A long history between the two California teams continues in a heated preseason rivalry.

San Diego, CA, February 19- With Major League Soccer's official opening day less than one week away, San Diego Sol looks for the win against long-time rivals in their last friendly of the season. Head Coach, James Calder, enthusiastically looks forward to the meeting between teams.

James is quoted as saying, "As we continue to grow our presence in the league, we are continually looking for ways to improve our overall fitness and success as a team. With a prosperous training regime over the last several weeks, I am confident in the team's ability to play a full ninety minutes against LA Galaxy."

END RELEASE

CLIMBING onto the bus along with the rest of my team, I quickly take a seat near the front of our transportation as we wait for the coaching staff to join us. Music swirls in the air around the bus as the guys get settled, propping pillows against windows and opening snacks for what should be a quick trip to Los Angeles. Cole takes the two seats next to me, and as we wait for the symbolic start of the new season to roll out of the lot much like the bus we're on, I can't help but think back to the times he and I have shared over the years on buses much like this.

"Hey," I grab his attention, not sure where this sentimental side has come from, "if you had to do it all over again, would you?"

"Fuck yeah, man. And not just for the cash or broads, either. We're among an elite few who get to do what they truly love every day. Isn't that life's ultimate goal?"

I don't answer, silently contemplating his words as the coaching staff climb aboard the bus and takes their seats.

Eleanor, distracted by her phone, slides into the seats directly in front of me, and I can't help but feel that if she would have noticed me, she would have chosen almost any other open spot on the bus. In lieu of her normal uniform of joggers and a t-shirt, she is wearing clingy black leggings that hug her thick thighs and an almost too-tiny tank emblazoned with our team logo, tits nearly spilling out the top. Her hair is still damp, hanging loosely around her face, and I have the damndest need to reach out and pull on one of those curls to get her attention.

But I don't.

Things have continued to be tense between us, and ever so slowly, it's starting to fuck with my brain. However friendly she is with the rest of the team, she has been giving me a wide berth since our altercation after her yoga class. In return, I've stopped actively looking for ways to make her life hell, only taking opportunities as they present themselves instead of seeking them out. Luckily for me, they still seem to present themselves almost daily. It's like a demented little game of cat and mouse where I continue to push and pull against her wherever I can while she tries desperately to get me to comply with her methods of training.

I've found myself obsessing over our conversation after her first day teaching yoga to the team, wondering what she meant when she said that I'd be rid of her for good after this season. Speaking that day, she acted like she wanted nothing to do with this team, with soccer–Hell, even with her dad. But then, the very next morning, she was the first one in the locker room, talking with several guys about how they were feeling after their session and preparing them for what was on their schedule for the day. Continually, I try to wrap my head around what she is doing here, and continually, I fail to make the connection between her and this team.

We're on the road for almost an hour before the chatter around us mostly calms down enough that I can turn the volume down on my audiobook to a respectable level. I crane my neck back, looking at my mostly sleeping teammates around me before looking in front of me to the wild, red curls sticking between the velour fabric of the seat backs in front of me.

Standing under the guise of a stretch before leaning my forearms on her seat back, I lean down as she types away on her phone.

"Excited for your first bus trip with the team, Princess?"

She jumps, her phone flying from her hand to land on the empty seat next to her. As she moves to pick it up, I'm able to see the screen, and when I read it–call me a snoop if you want–my brow furrows.

The text is addressed to someone named Jeff, a picture of what looks like Eleanor and a man set as the contact photo.

Eleanor: *What the fuck is a friendly? The staff keep talking about it.*

Jeff: *You really are clueless. It's the match your team is going to play tomorrow.*

Eleanor: *Thanks for the vote of confidence, jackass! I thought this was pre-season?*

Jeff: *It is. Did you forget your copy of Soccer for Dummies at home?*

Eleanor: *I've got the book in my bag and plan to do some more studying tonight.*

Jeff: *You've got this.*

No less than a hundred different questions are on the tip of my tongue.

Who is Jeff, and why is he important to Eleanor?

Is he a lover?

Was she with him while she was fucking me?

Why is she asking about our game like she has absolutely no idea what is happening?

Does she really have a copy of *Soccer for Dummies* in her overnight bag?

And most importantly, why the fuck do I care about any of the answers?

She switches off her phone screen before turning herself backward, her back propped against the seat backs in front of her, legs crossed on her seat. She crosses her arms over her chest, and I unabashedly swipe my gaze from her face, down to her killer cleavage, before returning to meet her green, kaleido-scope eyes.

Defiance flits over her face. "Does it really matter?"

Oh, she truly is a brat.

"I suppose it doesn't, Eleanor."

"It's Elle."

"Okay, Eleanor."

I return my ass to my seat, place my earbuds back in, and close my eyes as Stephen King's *Misery* narrates the rest of my journey.

Truly, a more apropos description of my current situation doesn't exist.

SINCE ARRIVING IN LOS ANGELES LESS THAN FORTY-eight hours ago, I've barely had a second of downtime to spend on my own. Between team dinners and spending the evening reviewing films of our opponents' previous year, to a morning training session followed by kicking the ever-living piss out of Galaxy on the pitch, it has been nothing but go, go, go. And it won't slow down until the season ends.

It's the large majority of the reason I decide to stay in at the hotel while most of the other guys head out to various bars and clubs during our small amount of downtime tonight. As much as I hate to admit it, my age is catching up with me, and there is nothing I want more in this moment than to slide into the rooftop hot tub while I let the stress of the day melt off my aching muscles.

I pull my board shorts up my body, tying them loosely around my hips before grabbing a towel from the bathroom. The top floor of the hotel that the team is staying at has been reserved specifically for us, and knowing there is someone posted outside the elevator, I skip a shirt, not worrying about running into anyone outside of my teammates and the security staff.

Deciding my body needs all the extra cool down that I am willing to give it after the grueling day, I opt to take the stairs up one story, pushing open the door to find a deserted pool, lowly lit by giant orbs floating along its surface. Slow, sensual jazz music flits across the cool February breeze as steam wafts into the air from the oversized hot tub strategically placed behind foliage at the far side of the roof.

As I approach the smaller pool of liquid heat, anxious to relax my tired muscles, I notice a figure sitting alone in the water. It only takes a nanosecond for my brain to register Eleanor's wild hair, piled tall on top of her head. Her eyes are closed, head back against the concrete of the in ground jacuzzi, a small, relaxed smile playing on her lips.

In her own little world, she hasn't noticed, me and I'm thankful for the opportunity to study her while she sits unaware and carefree. As infuriating as her attitude is, her beautiful body is equally just as maddening, and I don't miss the way my dick grows hard in my shorts as I take in her scantily clad body hovering just below the surface of the water.

I drop my towel on a nearby lounge chair and quietly make my way to the edge of the water. "Mind if I join you?"

Her eyes slowly drift open, almost as if she were just waking up. "I think that's the longest you've ever managed to remain silent in your life. I was wondering how long you were going to stand there before you spoke up."

Slowly, I descend the stairs, allowing my aching body to acclimate to the extreme change in temperature. Sitting across from Eleanor, I allow myself to slide down into the water, submerging my shoulders. Her eyes stay on me the entire time, a mixture of lust and need swirling across them as she roams her view over my chest and down to the low-slung board shorts clinging to my hips.

That's new.

"When did you know I was up here?"

She shoots me a sly grin. "I'm a single woman alone in a hotel at night, in a city I'm not super familiar with. I'm always well aware of my surroundings. If the sound of the door to the rooftop opening didn't alert me, surely the feeling of your eyes fixed on my tits would have."

I can't help but chuckle as I raise my hands in mock surrender. "Guilty as charged."

We sit in a comfortable silence for several minutes, the bubbles and jets of the jacuzzi providing us with a separate symphony from the music filling the rest of the outdoor space. Eleanor brings her arms out of the water, resting them along the wall of the hot tub, and I watch as the steam wafts off her skin before dissipating into the cool night air.

Weighing my words, trying to find a way to break the silence, I'm about to speak when Eleanor beats me to the punch.

"I don't know why you hate me so much. I'm not the person you make me out to be, Jay."

She sounds defeated, nothing like the spitfire of a woman who is never afraid to go toe-to-toe with me.

And for some reason, it tugs at a deeply hidden crevice of my soul that I've been burying for years, shattering the resolve I have to stay away from Eleanor Bigsby.

I should get out of the water, should get as far away from her as I can–preserve my dignity and any self-respect I have before this woman makes me do something I regret.

But of course, I don't leave.

I do the exact opposite.

Standing in the waist-deep water, I move until I'm in front of her. A hurricane of uncertainty fills her gorgeous eyes as I reach out to her hair, pulling the elastic securing the strands until they tumble down around her in unruly corkscrews. "The only reason I hate you is because every fucking time I look at you, I can't help but think back to how good it felt to be inside of you and how fucking gutted I was when I walked out of my bathroom and found you had left me alone."

Her eyes go wide, the smallest gasp entering into the air between us as I run my hands through her tangled hair. "I've wanted to pull you into an empty room every day since and demand you tell me why you ran, demand you strip down bare for me and let me touch you and taste you again."

I place a knee on the seat between her thighs, using my leverage to push her legs wider. Bringing my lips to hers, I lay one kiss against her silken mouth.

"Jay…" She moans my name when I pull away.

"Don't worry, Princess. I'm going to give you what you need, and while I do, you're going to tell me everything I want to know about the type of woman Eleanor Bigsby actually is."

Stepping back, I pull her with me until she is standing. Instructing her to turn around, I gently position her body so she is kneeling, thighs apart, on the smooth bench of the hot tub where she was just sitting moments before.

"What are you doing?"

Playing one hell of a beautiful game, I think to myself.

I don't answer her with words though. Instead, I bring my chest flush against her back, pushing her forward until I hear her gasp. "You don't cum tonight until I tell you that you can, do you understand that?"

She's breathy and needy as she nods her head and simultaneously moves her body, trying to direct the deep pressure of the jet from the hot tub against her clit.

"Who is Jeff?" While meant to be a question, it comes out as more of a demand.

"My brother."

"So, not someone you are seeing?"

"Na...no." She stammers the words as I grind into her from behind. "I'm not seeing anyone. Haven't for a very long time."

I exhale a breath I didn't know I had been holding, keeping her in place.

"Did you get this job because you're daddy's little girl?"

"No. I...I don't even like soccer. He said I had to work for the team for one year before I would have the knowledge needed to go work for the NFL. That's where I really want to be."

Stilling behind her, I allow her words to sink in, all the while allowing the stream of water to pulsate over her sex.

Eleanor begins to squirm, "Jay, I...I'm too close. I'm...I'm going to..."

"No, you're not." I pull her back from the jacuzzi's jet as she protests. "And it's Jensen to you." I lick up the side of her neck. "I like the way it sounds as it rolls off your tongue. Almost as much as I liked the way your tongue felt on my cock when you did that little trick with the condom last time we were together."

Trailing my hands over the curves of her body, I settle on her hips, pushing her back against the jet.

"Oh...oh, my God."

"Too much for you, baby girl?"

Bringing myself as close to her flesh as I can, I turn her head toward me crushing my lips to hers. Goddamn, I didn't realize how much I missed her lips.

Eleanor's body starts to tremble, and I pull her from the jet, delaying the gratification she so desperately wants. "Jensen, please, I'll tell you anything you want to know."

She starts, and it's like a dam has burst wide open. All the while, I continue to taunt and tease her body with slow, languid strokes along her skin.

"My parents adopted me when I was five. My birth mother loved The Beatles–that's why I'm Eleanor, and my sister is Michelle. She died shortly after giving birth to me, and the Bigsby's adopted us several years later when we became too much for our elderly grandparents. All my life, I've been made fun of because now I'm Eleanor Bigsby. It's a joke I can't escape."

I chuckle and reward her by pushing her back in front of the jet. "Tell me more."

"I hate chocolate but love chocolate cake. My first car was a Geo Metro, and my first crush was Jimmy Suarez in third grade. I wanted to be a marine biologist until I went to my first NFL game and saw the players and coaches on the field..." She trails off, taking a deep inhale as she tries to stop herself from falling over the edge just as I pull her away from the jet.

"Not yet, Eleanor."

She whimpers, and it is such a pathetic noise that I almost take pity on her.

Almost.

Moving to push her in front of the water again, we both freeze when we hear the telltale click of the door opening across the expanse of the pool deck.

A voice calls out my name, and I recognize it as Cole, who must have just returned from his night at the bar. While the sounds of the jets and bubbles can hide our voice if quiet, I still lower my voice to a whisper. "Stay quiet, Princess, unless you want him to watch as you come undone."

As silently as possibly, I push her in front of the jet again. Eleanor tries to distance herself from the pulsing water, but I overpower her, holding her in front of the constant stream.

"Jay, you up here, mate?" Cole calls again from somewhere closer.

Her entire body tenses against mine, her knees shaking as she struggles to hold herself up. Placing a flat palm in the middle of her back, I press her down until she is folded over the edge of the hot tub, pussy pressed as close to the jet as it can possibly get. "It sounds like he's coming closer, Princess, and I know that needy little cunt of yours is just begging for release."

I move my free hand to cover her mouth. "I remember how loud you are when you cum, but you're going to have to stay quiet tonight because, let's face it, while I love the idea of having others watch as you come undone, I'm a greedy fucking bastard, and tonight, I want that moment all to myself."

She trembles so hard against me, she may as well be riding one of those tacky mechanical bulls at a cowboy-themed night-club. I relish every small movement of her ass as it slides across my cock. "Come on; baby, it's time to let go. Cum for me before Cole reaches us."

And then somewhere between the wall of the jacuzzi and my body, she comes undone, bucking and thrusting her hips as she bites the palm of my hand to stifle the sounds of her orgasm.

Eleanor stills beneath me as the last of her release crashes over her, and I instinctively pull her into my arms, cradling her against my chest. Her own breathing comes deep, and she takes my hand in hers, turning it upward to place a kiss against the palm she bit. "I'm sorry for that."

"Yeah, what's that old idiom? Don't bite the hand that fingers you?"

Playfully, she smacks my chest, sending the sound of water splashing around us. "Somehow, I don't think that's how it goes."

I place another kiss on her lips because I can't get enough of her taste, just as Cole's footsteps reach us. Stilling for a moment, Eleanor quickly tries to move when it dawns on her that she is still in my lap, but I hold her to me, unwilling to let her go.

My friend's eyes dart between Eleanor and myself several times before a sly and knowing grin spreads over his face. "Sorry to interrupt."

"Don't lie–no you're not."

He barks out a laugh. "You're right, I'm totally not. Maybe wish I would have gotten here a few minutes earlier, though.

Anyway, I was just looking for you to let you know that it's almost curfew. Clearly, I now know why I couldn't get you on your mobile."

"I'll be down in a few."

Cole nods at me, giving a curt goodbye to Eleanor before turning and going back the way he came.

We sit in silence for a few minutes, much like when I first entered the water a short time ago. Finally, I turn Eleanor's face to mine. "Are we good?"

"Yeah, we're good."

She slides off me, reaching for my still rock-hard cock, but I grasp her hand. "Not tonight, Princess. We've gotta get back to our rooms."

Her smile turns to a mock pout, but she doesn't protest. Instead, we exit the hot tub together, and I help her towel off before she pulls a long dress over herself. It breaks my heart to watch her cover her body under so much fabric, but I don't protest.

Hand in hand, we walk back to her hotel room before parting ways with a kiss.

Halfway down the hall to my own room, I hear a door click, and when I turn towards the sound, Eleanor launches herself into my arms. She kisses me–again and again and again. "Goodnight, Jensen."

She turns, sauntering back to her room, and I watch her ass sway shamelessly the entire way.

SAN DIEGO SOL TO WELCOME LOCAL YOUTH CLUBS.

Soccer Daily Online: For Immediate Release

The team continues to expand grassroots work within their local community.

San Diego, CA, May 3- With strong bonds to the local San Diego community, the soccer club will welcome several underserved local youth clubs to practice on site alongside the San Diego Sol's youth academy.

Owner Maxwell Bigsby is quoted as saying, "We are forever fortunate to work with our local community and enjoy the time spent with the youth clubs from throughout San Diego. Having the ability to fund programs to train the future generations of star football athletes is a deeply personal mission that our team will continue to promote each year."

END RELEASE

As our season has progressed over the last few months, so has my relationship with the team–Jensen included. While we haven't so much as kissed since returning from Los Angeles, that night seemed to serve as a tipping point in our relationship. Where hatred and heated words once flowed so easily between us, we now maneuver through each day with a different set of dance steps. Conversation flows easily between us–playful words and heated gazes too.

I see the way he looks at me when he thinks no one else is paying attention. His eyes, such a light blue that they are almost translucent, have a way of sending shivers across my skin, even as the weather warms up in the last remaining days of spring.

It's how he's looking at me now as we sit around two tables that have been pushed together in the lunchroom, making enough space for the players, coaches, and Ophelia, who is never far behind.

"Explain it to me again?"

Groans break out around the table as I stare at my players and friend blankly.

Schmidt gestures to the salt and pepper shakers on the table, as well as the bottles of condiments strewn about. Setting the kitchen accouterments on the table in front of me as if they were players on the field, he explains for no less than the hundredth time, "A player is in an offside position if any portion of their head, body, or feet is in the opponent's half of the pitch *and* any part of their head, body, or feet is closer to the opponent's goal line than both the ball and the second to last opponent."

He moves the shakers around, demonstrating the gibberish he just spoke as if it is clear as day.

"Okay, now try explaining it to me like I'm five."

Two of the guys get up and leave, Cole is near to crying from laughing, and Coach Terry drops his head into his hands.

Ophelia pushes back from the table, standing abruptly. "I've got this."

All eyes fly to her, our little marketing maven, as she starts. "Pretend you're out at a club, and you see a super hot guy standing across the room." I don't miss how she glances over at Cole as she says the words.

"You're standing behind another woman, and from her body language you can tell you both have your eye on the same McBeefCake of a man. It just so happens that both you and this other woman left your phones at home, so you can't approach him and ask for his number."

She keeps going, "But you've got your fantastic wing woman of a best friend with you, and she throws you her phone so that you can get Hottie McHotPant's number.

"As soon as she has thrown you her phone and it has left her hands, you are able to slip around the other woman and get the guy's number. However, if you push around the woman and try to capture Sexy McStudMuffin's number before the phone has left your friend's hand, you would be offside and cannot get his number."

All around the table, wide eyes stare at Ophelia as she calmly sits back in her chair, crossing her feet at her ankles like a well-polished socialite.

I throw my hands up in exasperation. "Why the fuck didn't someone just explain it to me like that from the beginning?"

Everyone around the table laughs, and when I look at Jensen, a playful smile crosses his lips.

When I've finished eating, I take my tray to the counter, scraping off the leftovers into the trash before stacking my plate along with the others. I make it to the hallway, headed towards the small cubicle that serves as my desk in the training room, but Jensen catches up with me before I make it more than ten steps.

"Eleanor, wait up."

I glance at the smartwatch on my wrist. "I have to meet with Jasper in a few. We're working on getting him back in shape to play a full game."

"I won't keep you; I've got to get out to see the youth clubs that are here today. I just wanted to know if you had plans this weekend?"

Intrigued, but looking forward to a rare weekend without a game or travel, I answer honestly, "I plan to sleep for about twelve hours straight, binge Netflix, and sit on my couch for so long that the imprint of my fat ass is ingrained in the fabric by the time we come back to work on Monday."

His brow furrows, a deep crease forming between two perfectly sculpted eyebrows. "You shouldn't talk about yourself like that. Your ass isn't fat."

"Jensen, it's okay. I was just saying it as a figure of speech."

There is humor in my voice, yet the concern doesn't ebb from his features.

I've been a bigger girl my entire life. And while I still find it ridiculous that a size eighteen is considered "plus-sized," it's just a part of life that I've learned to deal with. In all honesty, I still have my days where I hate my body and resent the unfair beauty standards that plague women. I have days when I hate that I have to pay more for clothes than my skinnier friends simply because I am curvy, but more days than not, I absolutely love my body.

I love the way it's soft yet solid, curvy yet toned. I love how it bends and stretches, and I even have a small soft spot for the stretch marks that dot the side of my breasts.

"Oh…um, okay."

Now it is my turn to furrow my brow as I gaze at him slightly suspiciously. "What's up, Jay? Don't you have somewhere to be?"

"I want you to come over this weekend. Let me cook you dinner."

"I don't think that's the best idea."

"Why not?"

I sigh, debating if I should tell him the truth–tell him that it's a horrible idea because he can turn me to mush with a look, that he has been the star of too many of my recent fantasies, and that ever since that night in the hot tub, I touch myself almost nightly to thoughts of him, sometimes going as far as to shout his name into the empty abyss of my bedroom as I find my release, only to be more frustrated after I find it than I was beforehand.

I settle on a half-truth. "Because you seem to make my crazy show."

He laughs as a rakish grin spreads across his face, making him appear much younger than his thirty-four years. Jensen runs a hand over his mouth before scratching at the stubble currently lining his cheeks. "Well, Princess, I guess it is a good thing that I kind of like your crazy, isn't it?"

Reaching out, his fingers come to gently tug at one of the loose spirals that escaped my hair elastic. "Think about it, Eleanor. No false pretense– just dinner. Give me a chance."

"I'll think about it."

Nodding, he gives the same curl one last tug before releasing it and walking away, calling over his shoulder, "Text you tomorrow, Princess. I've got some kids to impress with my fancy footwork."

Already three minutes late for my next session of the day, I quickly tap out a text to Ophelia on my way to meet up with our rookie, who is recovering from minor knee surgery.

Eleanor: *SOS. What are you doing after work?*

Ophelia: *Going for two-for-one margaritas with my BFF!*

Ophelia: *Btw, you're my BFF.*

Ophelia: *If that wasn't clear, we're going for margaritas after work.*

Eleanor: *That sounds perfect. See you in the parking garage when I'm done.*

A few hours later, and after a quick change–thanks to the extra set of clothes I keep in my locker–I meet up with Ophelia, and we walk the few blocks to TacoCat, a local Mexican restaurant with more taco and margarita options than I can count.

Sitting across from me in a booth, Ophelia points to the cartoon logo of a cat wrapped in a taco shell. "Why do you think they call it TacoCat?"

"Probably because TacoCat spelled backwards is still TacoCat."

She seems to mull it over before responding proudly, "Yeah, and boobytrap spelled backward is partyboob!"

We both burst into laughter as our drinks are set down on the table.

The first and second margarita go down smoothly, perhaps a little smoother than they should, and I'm just starting on my third when I finally begin to confide in my friend. "Jensen wants me to come over for dinner this weekend."

"Girl, didn't I warn you on day one not to fall in love with one of them?"

I sputter at her accusation, margarita landing on myself and the table. "Who said anything about love?"

She looks at me skeptically over the rim of her larger-than-life margarita glass, licking the salt from the rim. "Do you like him?"

Sighing, I drop my head onto the table in front of us, my mind fuzzy from the river of tequila coursing through my system. "I'm still on the fence about him."

"Would you take off from work if he died?"

"Ophelia!" I straighten up, shocked by what she said.

"I'm serious, Elle. That's how I always gauge how into a guy I am. If I wouldn't take off work to go to his funeral, chances are, I'm not interested in anything serious."

Sucking down the last of the tequila in my glass, I contemplate her words. "How do you always make sense in the weirdest way?"

"You'd totally go to his funeral."

I reach for my next drink, thankful the bartender brings them two at a time. "Yeah, I would."

"So, go. Have dinner with him, but do it because it is what you want to do and not what he wants you to do."

She makes it sound so easy, and maybe it is. But deep inside, there is still a part of me that knows Jensen West has the ability to absolutely wreck me, and that terrifies me more than anything.

SAN DIEGO SOL PLAYERS SPOTTED AT LOCAL RESTAURANT INCOGNITO.

Gossip Nation Online: For Immediate Release

Local source claims both Jensen West and Cole Milner were spotted laying low while enjoying a casual dinner.

San Diego, CA, May 4- A local source spotted two of San Diego's most desired bachelors enjoying dinner on the down low at a local Mexican restaurant. Wearing casual clothing and baseball hats, they appeared to be hiding away from outside eyes. The duo enjoyed tequila with a side of tacos while sneaking peeks at two women at a nearby table.

The source, who wishes to remain anonymous, is quoted as saying, "Like...I know these guys are big dudes, bro, but you should have seen them tossing back shots. The only thing hotter than their tequila and taco bill was how hot the fine ass ladies were that they kept eyes on all night long."

Subsequent reports have stated local Mexican restaurant TacoCat is currently completely out of tequila with a new shipment arriving early next week.

END RELEASE

Shortly before 9:00 a.m., my phone wakes me up with a text notification. Head a little fuzzy from the numerous margaritas the night before, I grab the device from my nightstand, expecting to find a message from my sister or Ophelia.

Instead, a photo message is displayed on my screen–a gorgeous pool flanked by palm trees fills the background, and a charcoal gray yoga mat and oversized water jug are in the foreground.

Before I can respond, another message comes through.

Jensen: *I'm trying to practice what you preach, Princess.*

Eleanor: *For the love of God, Jay, it's not even nine.*

Jensen: *Maybe I'm just excited to start my day. Dinner tonight?*

I lay there for several minutes, phone still clutched in my hand as I debate the repercussions of dinner with Jensen. Going back over my conversation with Ophelia from the night before, I decide to throw caution to the wind and text him back.

Eleanor: *What time?*

He writes back within seconds. My heart hammers in my chest as I watch the text bubble appear on my screen.

We spend a few more minutes texting, settling on a time, and after he sends his address, I tell him I'll see him then before quickly dialing Michelle in a slight panic.

Way too chipper for a Saturday morning, she answers with

her usual greeting, singing me the first line of Eleanor Rigby. Even with my slight hangover, I respond, in turn, by singing a bit of Michelle in response.

"What's up, little sis?"

"You know, I've always hated how much of a morning person you are."

She chuffs out a laugh before I continue, "I need some advice, Michelle."

"Oh, sisterly advice! I've been waiting for this day since the day you were born."

Now, it is my turn to laugh.

"Come on! I've asked you for advice plenty of times! You helped me learn to surf, helped me decide which college to go to, talked me through way more than one bad breakup...you've always been there for me.

"Well, love, you've done the same for me more times than I can count. You might be my younger sister, but you give very sage advice, Elle."

I'm not sure about sage advice, but Michelle is right. As far as she and I go, we've always been there for each other, and I sometimes feel that if we weren't sisters, we would have found our way to each other as friends. We're fiercely protective of each other and extremely loyal, too.

"I agreed to have dinner with Jensen tonight."

She gasps. "The infamous player you work with who was also your one-night-stand, who then tormented you for weeks, who then got you off in a hotel hot tub using nothing but the stream of the jets?"

See? I can tell her anything without judgment. Even better, I know what I say to her will never get back to our parents. And with a situation like this–me hooking up with one of my dad's players multiple times–that is a necessity.

"The one and only," I respond.

"So, what advice do you need?"

"Don't judge me, but I'm meeting him at his house. He asked to cook dinner for me. But, like, what do I wear? Do I take a gift for him as a hostess present? He has an amazing pool. Is it too presumptuous to take my suit along? And what the hell do I do if he tries to sleep with me again?" Even though my sister can't see me over the phone, I count off each question on my fingers as I list them out loud.

Bless my sister, always one for being able to talk me off the ledge. With her help, I decide to wear a simple sundress, take a nice bottle of wine, my swimsuit will stay at my apartment, and if Jensen does try something, I'll play it by ear and see how I'm feeling about him in that moment.

I can't help but to replay my conversation with Ophelia from the previous night over and over again in my head as I go about my day. I wasn't lying when I said I was on the fence about Jensen. Clearly, there is something there, but I still don't know if it is purely physical or if something emotional could be happening between us, too. I've enjoyed getting to know him over the last few months. We've shared more about our lives, he's helped me become more comfortable with the sport of soccer, and I've even been able to get through to him with some new conditioning programs.

While my Saturday seems to drag on, I soon find myself in front of Jensen's door, suddenly reluctant to ring the bell. Of course, I should have guessed his house would be outfitted with one of those fancy doorbell cameras because as I stand in front of the door, debating if I should run, the oversized door swings open to reveal the man himself.

Although it's warm in the almost summer sun, he is wearing a pair of distressed denim jeans with several frayed holes along the thighs and shins. I do a double take at his tee, not expecting him to be the type of guy to wear a novelty shirt, but he does in fact have on a shirt that reads *Kicking It Old School* along with a pair of soccer cleats. Just a hint of his tattoos peek out from below the sleeves, and I momentarily feel lucky to know what he looks like under that shirt.

He grins, a lopsided little tilt of the corners of his mouth, and I swear it's enough to make my lady parts flutter.

We stand there for several seconds, taking each other in before he takes my free hand in his, bending forward to give me the softest kiss. Our lips barely touch, merely ghosting along one another. "You want to come in, or would you prefer we have dinner here on the front porch?"

It was dark the last time I was here, and my mind was so preoccupied that I didn't look at the marvelous house I was entering. This time, I follow him into the mansion, taking in my surroundings.

I grew up in large homes before choosing a simple one-bedroom apartment for myself after college. Still, none of those places are anything as incredible as this.

The foyer is large and open, allowing natural light to pour in from all around. I can already see hints of the Pacific off in the distance. For someone like Jensen, who can be so cold when he feels wronged, I expected his house to be full of dark wood and deep colors. Instead, the living room is open and airy with a beachy vibe. Filled with beiges and blues, a large, upholstered sectional fills the space while a huge piece of driftwood hangs from the ceiling, doubling as a chandelier.

Looking up at it, I don't even realize I'm talking out loud. "This is stunning."

Jensen is still next to me, my hand still in his. "Isn't it? The wood is manzanita. It had washed up after a bad storm a few years ago. I let it sit on the beach for a few days, and every time I walked past it, I knew I wanted to do something with it, but wasn't sure exactly what. So, I hauled it to the garage, and it sat there for a few weeks before I brought up the idea to Cole. It was actually his idea to turn it into a light."

"You guys are close, aren't you?"

He nods as he leads me into the kitchen where pans are already on the stovetop with something delicious-smelling simmering in them. "Aye. We've been mates since we were young lads. Played quite a bit together at home before we both came to the states to play for MLS."

Home.

I hadn't thought about it until now, that California isn't Jensen's home, that one day, he might decide to return to the UK and leave the states altogether. The thought sends an odd chill over my body–achill that he of course notices.

After stirring something on the stove, he comes to stand in front of me, rubbing his large hands up and down my arms. "Cold?"

"Must have been a ghost."

He chuckles, and I like the way it sounds. I *really* like the way it sounds. "A ghost, eh?"

I nod in response. "Just something my grandmother used to say. She always said when a chill would go over your body quickly, that it was a ghost stopping by to say hello."

"I like that sentiment."

Jensen moves back to the stove, stirring our meal. "Hey, can I get you something to drink?"

"Oh, hold on!" I had forgotten all about the bottle of wine tucked into my large tote bag. I walk to the kitchen stool where I had placed my bag, pull out the bottle of white wine, and bring it back to where he stands. "I brought you a gift. Just a little something for having me."

"That was sweet of you. I'll pop it in the freezer for a few minutes to chill. Want to join me and have a glass? It is a special occasion."

"And what's that occasion?"

That addictive laugh is back again, and I find myself wishing I could bottle it up in a little glass jar. I'd carry it in my purse, opening it up whenever I was sad for an instant boost of serotonin. "I got you here for dinner. That's a special enough occasion for me."

I can't help the smile that spreads across my face. And just when I think Jensen West can't get any sweeter, he tucks a stray curl behind my ear, leans in close, and whispers, "I haven't told you yet just how beautiful you look today, Eleanor. But you truly do. You always do."

I'm sure I'm full-on blushing now, managing a quiet thanks in response.

Somehow, I manage to regain my composure. "What are you making? Anything I can help with?"

"Decided to treat you to one of my favorite comfort foods—steak and ale pie with a homemade pastry and steak gravy. And I'm good, Princess. Want to grab the wine from the freezer and pour us each a glass?"

Under Jensen's direction, I find two wine glasses in a cabinet, bring them to the island, and uncork the wine after removing it from the freezer. I begin to pour as he starts plating our meals, surprised at how natural it feels to be working in tandem with him. I turn toward him, wine glass in each hand. "Want me to take these to the table?"

Pointing to a sliding glass door with a spatula, Jensen asks, "What do you think about eating out on the patio?"

I take a sip from my glass, enjoying the crisp grape and citrus flavor as it slides down my throat. "I can't think of a better idea. Let me set these down, and I'll come back to help."

"No need. I'll be right behind you."

Maneuvering my way through the sliding door proves to be challenging with a wine glass in each hand, but I successfully manage to make my way to the patio without spilling a drop. Setting our glasses down on a small bistro table, I walk across the brick-paved patio, bypassing the stunning pool to look out at the gorgeous blue water in front of me. The sounds of the waves crashing on the shore are soothing, and I can hear the gentle laughter of children coming from further down the beach. A gentle breeze wafts across the air, and when I look skyward, I see two kites flying off in the distance.

I don't hear Jensen when he comes out to the patio. Rather, I feel his presence as he comes to stand behind me. "It's beautiful, isn't it?"

"It really is," I say, my voice coming out thready as I turn to face him.

His eyes lock on mine, and I swear, they're bluer than any ocean in the world, including the one in front of us.

We've been playing this game of back-and-forth for months–one minute being nice to each other, the next, at each other's throats–but, in this moment, standing in front of him with the Pacific as our backdrop, I know without certainty that Jensen West has a piece of me that I'll never get back.

Linking his fingers through mine, he leads me back to the table that now holds our wine as well as two large white plates almost overflowing with food. Jensen pulls out my chair, pushing it back in once I'm situated, before placing a cloth napkin across my lap with a wink. The aroma of the food makes my mouth water–a rich, meaty smell with a hint of hops.

After sitting next to me, he holds out his glass. "I know we didn't get off on the right foot, or rather, we got off on the exact right foot before taking one hell of a detour, but I'm happy you are here with me tonight."

I lift my drink to his, the clinking of our glasses echoing against the backdrop of gently-crashing ocean waves before we both pick up our forks to enjoy our meal.

MYSTERY WOMAN SPOTTED VISITING SOL STAR JENSEN WEST'S HOME.

Gossip Nation Online: For Immediate Release

Playboy soccer star appears to be off the market, welcoming the woman with a gentle kiss.

San Diego, CA, May 5- After a night of voracious tequila shots, playboy soccer star, Jensen West, appears to have entertained a mystery woman at his Pacific coast home.

The anonymous source we spoke with yesterday confirms the mystery woman is the same voluptuous, red-headed woman West was watching from afar at the restaurant.

Story developing.

END RELEASE

ELEANOR LOOKS beautiful tonight in a low-cut, yellow sundress and strappy little sandals, but then again, she looks beautiful in everything she wears. She was gorgeous the first night I met her at City Syn, stunning when I surprised her on the first day of training, and a total knock out in her tiny little two-piece bathing suit in Los Angeles. But right now, as she closes her lips around her fork and lets out a moan of appreciation at my cooking, she is absolute perfection.

There have been times she has driven me absolutely bonkers, like when she slapped me or when she is twisting my body into a pretzel while trying to teach me some crap yoga pose, but there hasn't been one moment that I haven't found myself wildly attracted to her.

"This really is wonderful," she says before taking another bite. "How did you learn to cook like this? Did your mom teach you?"

"No, I actually didn't have a lot growing up. I have a brother and three sisters, so food was almost always scarce."

Eleanor looks at me, and I momentarily tense, expecting to see pity. But it isn't pity I see reflected back at me in her large, green eyes. It's empathy. And that empathy has me continuing with my story. "After I signed my first professional contract, I bought my first house and hired a chef. But I wanted to be able to fend for myself and not have to rely on anyone, so she started to teach me some of the traditional English recipes. Bangers and mash, toad in the hole…"

Her laughter cuts me off. "I'm sorry–did you say toad in the hole?"

"Sure did, Princess."

"That sounds so bizarre!" She's still giggling, wiping at a stray tear that escaped through her laughter.

"Might sound bizarre, but it is absolutely delicious." We might be talking about food, but I can't help but look down to glance at her lips, which are equally as delicious as any food I've ever tasted.

"I don't think I could ever eat it. Is there actually *toad* in it?"

She is completely unaware how beautiful she is when she's like this–uninhibited and free as she laughs with me. "Nah, no toad. It's actually sausages enveloped in a giant Yorkshire pudding–which isn't actually pudding and more of a pastry–and drizzled in gravy. *But*, if you think that name is bizarre, you surely haven't heard of bubble and squeak or singing hinnies."

"Stop it!" she squeals, bursting out into yet another fit of laughter.

The grin on my face is so wide that it physically hurts. "I will do no such thing. And let's not forget about the staple British dessert of spotted dick."

"Jensen! You're totally fucking with me!"

"Swear on my life." I make the sign of the cross over my chest.

"I'm not sure I'm brave enough to even ask…" she trails off.

A low rumble escapes me. "It's a traditional steamed pudding filled with chopped currants and drizzled with a glutto-nous vanilla custard sauce. It's wonderful and one of my favorite desserts."

Eleanor finishes the last bite of food on her plate, and an odd sense of pride envelopes me knowing she liked my food enough to eat an entire plate. I love that she doesn't shy away from food, that she isn't some prissy California socialite that cuts carbs or counts calories while surviving on a diet of wilted lettuce and water with lemon. She's a real woman–maybe the first one I've known since relocating to California–and I can't get enough of her.

"I think I'm just going to have to take your word for that. It's not that I'm not an adventurous eater, but I don't think I could eat something called spotted dick. Just...ew." She closes her eyes and shakes her head as she says it, her curls bouncing around wildly.

"Guess it's a good thing that's not what's on the menu for dessert, eh?" I stand, taking her plate, and she stands, too. "Stay. Enjoy the view. I'll be right back."

"Is it okay if I put my feet in the pool 'til you come back out?"

"What's mine is yours, Princess."

Eleanor walks to the edge of the pool, kicking off her sandals. As I enter back into the house, I turn, watching as she gracefully sits on the edge of the pool, dropping her feet and legs into the water.

Quickly, I cut two large pieces of homemade cake and grab two forks, as well as the rest of the bottle of wine. Pausing before I return to the patio, I quickly detour to my room, changing from my jeans into a pair of loose basketball shorts.

Hearing me return, Eleanor starts to rise, but I stop her. Setting the dessert on the table where we ate, I grab a smaller side table and place it behind her before topping off our wine. I bring the glasses to the small table, followed by the cake. Finally, I sink to my knees before dropping my feet into the pool next to hers.

Turning to grab a plate, I hand it to her before taking the second for myself. She simply stares at the plate for a moment before looking over at me. "Hate chocolate, but love chocolate cake."

"How did you know that?"

Taking a bite of my cake, I pause before answering, knowing my next words could have her running for the door. "Hot tub confessions, babe."

A gorgeous blush spreads across her cheeks and across her chest. It's the fucking sexiest thing I've ever seen. "That night was…"

"Something special," I finish before she can.

We sit together in silence with our feet in the pool as we eat cake, watching the sun set off over the ocean in the distance. It's beautiful and peaceful, and for the first time in as long as I can remember, I'm not worrying about the future of my career, my tarnished reputation, or the many past mistakes I've made. I'm only thinking about the here and now and the beautiful woman next to me.

She sets her empty plate on the table and leans back, placing her weight on her arms.

"Want another piece?"

Patting her stomach with one hand, she responds, "Oh, Lord, no! I think you made me gain five pounds tonight. I'm going to need a serious workout after that meal."

I'm not sure what prompts me to do it, but I can't stop myself from reaching over, gently teasing her pinkie with mine. She doesn't pull away, but I can't help but notice how she visibly tenses.

She lets out a long sigh. "What are we doing, Jay?"

As seems to happen often in her presence–my body reacts before my brain has a chance to catch up, and I find myself sliding off the pool deck and into the waist-deep water. My shirt clings to me as the water quickly spreads upwards over the once-dry cotton fabric, but I can't be bothered by the way it molds to me like a second skin.

Eleanor has a look of pure shock on her face as I come to stand in front of her. Gently, I nudge her thighs apart until I am able to stand between her legs. I run my hands up her thighs, lightly teasing under the hem of her dress before continuing up to rest my palms on her hips.

"I want you, Eleanor, and I'm fairly confident that I've made that abundantly clear. You drive me absolutely mad and push every single one of my buttons. Hell, half the time, I don't know if I want to praise you or punish you, but I do know that I need to have you."

Her brows come together as she tenses, her lips pressing into a tight, straight line, and it kills me to see those conflicted feelings as they dance across her pretty face. "You could fuck any woman out there. I'm not anything special."

How does she not see how fucking special she truly is? It physically pains me that she does not see herself the way I do.

"Fuck, Princess. First, I never want to hear you say that you aren't anything special because you are nothing short of spectacular. Second, yes, Eleanor–yes I want to fuck you, but I want to do *so* much more. I want to truly get to know you. I want to take you on romantic dinner dates and fly you around the world in the off-season. I want to spend our days exploring the city and our nights exploring your fucking magnificent body. I want to spoil the absolute shit out of you just to see you smile. Because that smile–that fucking smile–it lights me up every damn time I see it."

If you were to look up dumbfounded in the dictionary at this very moment, you would see a picture of Eleanor Bigsby as the definition.

See also: astonished.

See also: bewildered.

See also: perplexed.

She sits like that for what seems like minutes, just staring at me as I continue to hold onto her hips with my large hands. Her exquisite, emerald eyes darting between my own, she finally speaks in a tone so hushed that it's almost a whisper. "You...you want to date me?"

I don't hesitate with my response. "Fuck yes, I want to date you."

Her head nods a few times like she is somehow still trying to wrap her head around what I just unloaded on her. "Can we even do that? I mean, we work together. I'm sure there is something about player and coach relationships being frowned upon."

"I already checked the player's handbook for the team. There isn't any mention of inter-office dating. Perhaps because the team has never had a female coach before. But I subscribe to the idea that it is better to beg for forgiveness later than ask for permission first."

"You're certifiable, Jensen. You seriously looked at the handbook? I didn't even know we had a handbook. Little confident, aren't you?"

"I wanted to have all my bases covered so I could be prepared for any pushback you gave me." I flash her the biggest grin ever, hoping my cheeky charm rubs off.

She giggles, that intoxicating little laugh that goes in equal parts straight to my heart and dick. I squeeze her hips, just firm enough to make her stop. "So, what do you say, Eleanor. Give me a chance?"

Her eyes close for a second, and she shakes her head as if trying to clear her mind before a giant smile breaks out across her face. "I haven't stopped thinking about you since the first night I met you. No one has ever made me feel so free and adventurous before, and I didn't know I was missing that until I met you. I'm scared shitless, Jensen, and I swear, if you hurt me, I'll have your balls on a silver platter, but yes. Yes, I'll give you a chance."

Without warning, she launches herself into the pool and into my arms. I stumble, caught off guard, and we both quickly drop under the cool water before coming up to the surface. Soaked from head to toe, our clothes hang off our bodies, Eleanor's crazy curls plastered to her face, we both have huge smiles on our lips. She loops her arms around my neck and her legs around my waist, my own personal little koala, before kissing me.

What starts out as gentle caresses of our lips quickly turns hungry as our tongues battle for possession within each other's mouths. Her hands are in my short hair, tugging and pulling on the strands, and I know she can feel how hard I've become between our bodies.

Pulling back, panting, she drops her forehead to mine before closing her eyes. Merely a whisper, her breath caresses my lips as she speaks. "Please don't break my heart, Jensen."

And then, as fast as she pulled away, her lips return to mine, the passion in my fiery redhead finally reignited.

CECELIA VAN HUTCHINSON SPOTTED IN SAN DIEGO AFTER US TOUR.

Gossip Nation Online: For Immediate Release

Previously linked to soccer's resident bad boy, Jensen West, Van Hutchinson is the apparent leak of the previously released naked pictures of the star.

San Diego, CA, May 6- Following a semi-successful leg of her US tour, Cecelia Van Hutchinson has returned to San Diego. The social media influencer turned model turned pop star has reportedly been in talks with several networks while looking for a home for her new reality television show, Help! I Almost Married A Professional Athlete.

Cecelia Van Hutchinson is quoted as saying, "While the television show will follow real life individuals who made the ultimate mistake of marrying a professional athlete, I can one hundred percent say any relationship I have with a professional athlete has been nothing but wonderful. In fact, I am looking forward to reuniting with Jensen in the coming weeks."

END RELEASE

ELEANOR

10.

I HAVE no idea how much time passes as Jensen and I kiss. Minutes, hours–hell, days could have passed, and I'd be none the wiser. I'm only aware of our bodies pressed together, arms wrapped around one another, and lips fused between us as we stand in the shallow end of the pool.

All I know is that I've been craving this moment since we first kissed all those months ago at the club, and now, I never want it to end.

But, of course, all too soon it comes to an end when Jensen pulls his lips from mine. Leaning into me, he presses his forehead against my own, his hands still moving over my body, both above and below the warm water that surrounds us. "You truly have no idea how sexy you are, do you, Eleanor?"

Feeling my cheeks heat under his simple praise, I pull away, allowing myself to bury my head into his shoulder. But this only fuels him on. "I can't count the number of times I've missed a pass during training because I'm too busy staring at you. That absolute sitter of a shot against Philadelphia? Yeah, missed it because I saw you on the sideline helping to run the guys through some warm-ups. You were bent over, and your ass looked utterly delectable in the shorts you had on. I was so transfixed by you that I didn't see the ball coming right at me."

This has me laughing into the crook of his neck. "You're so full of shit."

"Mmmm…and that filthy mouth of yours. Don't even get me started."

I giggle again, hoping to stop his onslaught of confessions, but he isn't finished yet.

"Serious, Elle. That first night, the things you said–fuck, it took it to a whole new level. I never met a woman who was so confident in what she wanted, in how you all but demanded to be treated like a dirty little fuck-toy. It was next-level hot."

Somehow, his dirty words spur me on, giving me a jolt of confidence that makes me open my mouth. He likes it dirty; he likes *me* dirty, and I want to give him what he likes because honestly, it's exactly what I've always wanted, too. "Jensen."

"Yes?"

I raise my head, just enough to be level with his ear. Arms still wrapped around his neck, I run my fingers up into his hair, gently teasing and tugging on the strands as they weave through my hands. "You should see what else I can do with this filthy mouth of mine."

A low growl reverberates through his body as he takes clumsy steps across the shallow water. Jensen keeps me in his arms, my legs wrapped around his sturdy frame as he ascends the concrete stairs of the inground pool, not stopping when we reach the top. Strong arms envelope my body, not coming off me until we're inside and he is gently setting me down on his bed.

As he looks at me, I look around the familiar room, taking more time to appreciate the dark yet stunning view that follows my line of sight. His bedroom is sparsely decorated in comparison to what I saw earlier in the rest of his house, but knowing now what I do about Jensen's past, it makes sense to me that he would hold onto possessions like recipes and relationships in lieu of physical possessions like artwork or belongings.

Taking my hand in his, he tugs me into a standing position

before reaching down to drag my soaked dress up and over my head. Dropping it to the ground without fanfare or show, it makes an audible *thwack* as it lands against the tile floor.

The air is cool against my skin, sending shivers over my still-damp body.

But I don't mind.

I don't mind when I see the adoration and awe in which Jensen looks at me.

I don't mind when his large palms cup my breast over the thin fabric of my bra.

I don't mind when that same bra drops to the ground between us after he deftly works the clasp and slides it down my arms.

Seconds later, he slides my panties down my lower half, urging me to spread my legs to allow the fabric to fall to the ground around my feet when they momentarily cling to my thick thighs.

And that quick, the adoration and awe is gone, a crazed, hungry man standing before me in his place.

He makes a slow loop around me, like a shark circling his prey before moving in for the kill. I'm that prey, completely at his mercy, and the thought sends a jolt of lust straight through my body.

A single finger trails painstakingly slow from the bottom of my spine to the top of my neck.. I unintentionally suck in a breath, holding it in with anticipation. Still behind me, his fingers tangle in my hair, brushing all the wet strands behind my shoulders and creating a makeshift ponytail before he returns to stand in front of me.

Jensen's voice is low and deep, deeper than I've ever heard, as he speaks to me, holding my gaze with his own now icy blue eyes. "Are you ready to show me what that filthy mouth can do?"

I'm barely able to rasp out a breathy *yes* before his lips are on mine, plundering my mouth with his own. Pulling away from me, almost like it torments him to do so, he strips his still wet shirt from his body, discarding it on the floor next to my dress. "Then get on your knees for me, Princess."

A gentle hand lands on each shoulder, guiding me down to my knees. I quickly acquiesce his demand, the cold tile biting against my already sensitive skin. He starts to take his pants off, but I stop him with my hand on his. "Let me."

Jensen gives me an imperceptible nod before bringing both of his palms up, linking them behind his head with a smirk. It makes his already solid body flex in ways I never imagined possible, all hard abs and pecs, and all on display for me. I see this man training five days a week, sometimes more. I see him on the field, outrunning and outshooting men nearly half his age, yet I've never seen him like this–like an absolute God, the kind of God chiseled out of marble that was worshiped throughout ancient history and still celebrated the world around. I can't help but reach out my palms, ghosting them down his stomach with the lightest of touches. His abs contract under my graze as I slowly continue my assault downward where I tuck my fingers underneath the band of his shorts.

His already hard cock is straining against the fabric, the outline taunting me. Unable to help myself, I bring my mouth to him, lightly caressing his dick through his shorts with my teeth as a groan pours from his mouth. "Christ, Eleanor–the things you do to my body."

"And to think," I say as I ease his shorts down inch by agonizing inch, "I'm just getting started."

Finally, I pull his shorts and briefs down. The wet fabric pools at his feet, partially covering my knees as well. The articles of clothing are cool, almost cold, but still, they do little to quench the heat rolling through my body.

Jensen's long, thick cock juts forward, taunting me much in the way I'm about to taunt him. Lowering my lips to him, I get my first true taste of his skin–a mixture of chlorine, musk, and just a hint of salt. It's heady and arousing and instantly has me lowering my lips further, anxious to take him as fully as I can into the warmth of my mouth.

I lick and suck my way up and down his shaft, slowly taking more and more of him into my mouth each time I crest over the tip. And each time he starts to relax, I pull back, starting the sweet torture all over again. I smirk, feeling his body tense again and this time, I reward him with my short nails gliding down the front of his thighs as I take him in just a little deeper than before.

He groans when I pull my lips from him again, and I playfully look up through my lashes, feigning innocence as I tease him with my words. "What's wrong, Jay? Not a fan of edging unless you're the one in control of it?"

Heat flashes behind his eyes, his arms finally dropping from where they were firmly planted behind his head. One hand comes to tightly fist my hair, and the other gently slaps me several times across the cheek. "I told you before–to you, it's Jensen, *not* Jay. Now shut the fuck up and take what I have to give you."

God, he is *so* filthy. I love every second of it.

I lick my lips, allowing him to tilt my head where he wants with his tightly woven fingers. Placing me where he desires, he gently rubs his thumb over my lower lip before pressing the tip of his cock to my lips. "God, Eleanor, I can't wait to wreck your beautiful face with tears."

And with those dirty words, he pushes inside of my mouth, not wasting time before he is thrusting fully into me with long, punishing strokes of his dick. His pace is relentless, his hold on my hair enough to have tears already pricking at my eyes. Yet still, I want more.

Reaching behind him with my hands, I grip his ass, digging my nails into his skin, silently asking for more. Obliging my request, he drops my tresses from his hand, bringing one palm to each side of my face. Holding me between his hands, he pushes and pulls my face to him as he does the same with his hips..

His balls slap off my chin, and I should be ashamed–horrified–at this crude act, but all I can think is how much I want it, how much I want him–all of him–in this wild abandon where I give all of me and he takes all of it in return. Somehow in this weird, sick, twisted world of degradation that I love and crave, I feel safe with Jensen.

I want to take him deeper, want to feel him all the way in the back of my throat as he thrusts, and when I feel him hit my gag reflex, I only momentarily lose my movements until I swallow him down with his next thrust, taking him deeper than I've ever taken any man before.

He pumps and thrusts, over and over and over again before he suddenly pulls out as spit trickles from my mouth. Fingers back in my hair, he pulls me to my feet as a small moan escapes me. His lips are on me–hard–as he kisses me before biting my lip, then down my neck and across my shoulder. "Can you handle more, Love?"

I know it's nothing but an English term of endearment, still I can't help but love hearing it tumble off his tongue in the heat of the moment. It's soft and delicate, an extreme contrast to the way he treats my body when we're being intimate. And I like it...a lot.

Panting and moaning against him, I answer truthfully, "I can handle anything you give me."

Pushing me back down, only his soggy shorts cushion my knees as I fall against the hard tile. Without warning, he's back in my mouth, gagging me on the sudden intrusion. Tears do fall now, not from pain or embarrassment because trust me, I want this *just* as much as he does. I crave both sides he has shown he can give me–the gorgeous, thoughtful dinners as well as the sexy, dominant, and dirty fun we can have together. No, these tears fall from a mixture of pure wild abandonment, lust for this man that stands before me, and for the need to have every single piece of him that he is willing to share with me.

I'm gagging on his length, choking on every thrust of his warm skin as it intrudes my throat. I'm a melting pile of hot need, and I reach between my legs, desperate to touch myself, but his hand comes to stop me, pulling my arm away from my body. "No. You don't get to touch yourself until you finish me off. Maybe if you're a good girl for me and you swallow every last drop of my cum, maybe then I'll let you touch yourself while I watch."

I whimper around his cock, but he doesn't relent. Instead, he brings the hand that had just moved mine away from my clit up to my face, and wipes at the tears that are running down my face with his thumb. "You look so beautiful when you're ruined, Eleanor. I think I'd only prefer it more if you weren't wearing waterproof mascara so I could truly watch those tears streak your gorgeous, porcelain skin."

And then, with his cock still deep in my throat, he brings that hand to his mouth and licks my salty tears from his thumb all the while maintaining eye contact with me as I kneel on the ground in front of him, worshiping his cock with my mouth.

It's all I can do to stop myself from pressing my slick thighs together, chasing any minuscule ounce of pressure I can find. I want him between my legs– with his fingers, or tongue, or cock. The delivery doesn't matter, as long as he is there–and there soon.

Snaking my hand between his body, I gently roll his balls in the palm of my hand before lightly tugging down on them. 'm rewarded with a guttural groan as Jensen's hands once again come to wrap tightly in my tresses.

Continuing to offer my mouth to him, he continues thrusting into me, over and over. Spit and drool are now spilling from my mouth with every thrust, dripping down my chin, over my bare breasts, and onto the floor between us. It mixes with the tears that have fallen, and while most would find it disgusting and macabre, I've never felt as beautiful as I do in this moment.

Jensen begins to tense in front of me, the telltale signs of his release bubbling to the surface. His body is rigid, his thrusts becoming more sporadic. He's close, so close I can already taste his release. Through gritted teeth, he sounds more animal than human when he speaks. "I'm going to come down that pretty little throat of yours, Love. You're going to drink me down, and you're going to know that as long as you're with me, this is the only cock that will touch those lips."

He grunts as he pounds into my mouth again. "The only cock that will fuck that tight cunt of yours."

Another grunt. "The only cock that will fill the tight hole of your ass as you scream into the abyss as I claim every piece of your body."

If words alone could make me orgasm, I'd be in a puddle of my own arousal right now.

Instead of me finding my own release, Jensen finds his, but not before one hand comes to hold my neck possessively while the other comes to clamp...over...my...nose.

All oxygen to my body is cut off as I struggle to swallow the cum exploding from his dick. I should be afraid, scared. But instead, it's like I'm watching my body while hovering above, watching myself as my eyes go wide, and tears start to fall again. He stills, the last of his climax spilling into my throat, and only when he is good and ready does he slide out of my mouth while still keeping my nose plugged. Momentarily, I struggle to breathe before remembering that my mouth is now free. I gasp oxygen into my starved lungs, still unable to move away from Jensen but knowing that even if I was able to move away from him, I wouldn't want to.

"Open up wide and show me."

I do as requested of me, sticking my tongue out as if I were at the doctor's office. He smiles a proud smile at me, and the smile alone is enough praise to make my insides turn to instant lava.

He releases my nose, turning his hand over to gently stroke my cheek with his knuckles. I lap up the touch like a kitten, nuzzling my head further into his hand until he turns it over, granting me his entire palm.

I'm not sure what I expect of him next. All I know is that it wasn't what he does. Dropping to his knees in front of me, uncaring of the saliva and tears mixing together on my body and the floor around us, he pulls me into an embrace, kissing up and down my neck as he runs his hands over my body. "That was wonderful; you were wonderful. You're so dirty, so filthy, and I absolutely adore it, Love. Just promise me one thing, Eleanor. Don't run this time. If you need to talk through things, talk through them with me. If you need something from me, all you have to do is ask. Just–please don't run this time."

His voice is gruff yet earnest with a hint of vulnerability, but before I can respond to his request, he has me up and off the ground. He cradles me in his arms so effortlessly, as if I'm a feather, and walks us the several paces to his bed with ease.

As if I'm the most precious cargo in the world, he lays me down on top of the plush blankets adorning his mattress before crawling his way up my body, his already half-hard cock dragging against my skin.

Jensen's lips caress mine, his fingers working up and down my body, leaving no inch of my skin untouched by his ministrations. The juxtaposition between the wild animal of a man who was using me for pleasure just minutes ago and this soft gentleman treating my body with the utmost respect is jarring in the very best way.

"God, yes," I moan into his mouth.

Every single kiss, every nip and lick, every touch and caress from him is like a firework igniting across my skin, and I'm so desperate for more that it isn't beneath me to beg for it in this moment.

"Jensen, please!" I plead with him, needy for release. My voice is alien as it leaves my body, a voice I've never heard myself make before–husky and raw, like I've been screaming for hours. "I need you. Please don't make me wait any longer!"

"Oh, Love, I'll give you everything you want. You just need to ask for it."

Suddenly, I'm overcome by shyness. I want to shield myself away from his lustful gaze, but when I try to move for a blanket, he stops me. "Oh, no, there is no hiding from me now, Eleanor. I know you can use your words, little toy, so use them."

I'm silent for several more seconds, his hand drifting down to rest between my legs. Excruciatingly light, he drags one digit over my clit while speaking directly into my ear, his English accent like a balm to my soul. "You're my beautiful, *filthy*, incredibly *sensual* woman. I never wanted a woman before I met you, Eleanor–never wanted a woman for more than one night. And it is because of so much more than what you do in this bedroom with me, but Christ does it turn me on when you let inhibition go and tell me exactly what you want. So, tell me, my beautiful Princess. How can I make *you* feel as good as you just made me feel?"

I'm already needy from the gentle circles he's tracing on my clit, my body pulsing with desire and a dripping mess from every single kiss he's given my lips, lick he's given my skin, and thrust of his cock deep inside my throat.

"I want..." I stutter, trying to get to words out, "I want you to fuck me."

He slides his one, solitary digit further, probing my entrance. "Keep going."

"I want to feel you inside of me."

His finger dips inside my pussy. "What else?"

"I want to ride you. I want to feel your hands on my hips with punishing force as I undulate back and forth on top of you."

Another finger sinks in next to the first. "Yes, Love. Tell me all your dirty fantasies."

"Want you to fill my cunt, and my ass, and my mouth." My sentences are almost gibberish now, coming out without thought or concern for the English language.

A third finger joins the two already deep inside my pussy as Jensen thrusts and torments me, breaking me apart from the inside out. "Oh, and fill you, I will."

Without warning, he rolls on the bed, moving to lay beneath me, one leg straddled over each of his hips. His fingers are still inside me, still moving in a tantalizing back and forth and back and forth movement. Even just the sensation of his fingers makes me feel full, and I can't wait to have more.

"Stop teasing me and fuck me already!" My voice bounces off the barren walls of Jensen's room, amplifying the noises I'm making into our own private surround sound.

Wet fingers slurp as they are pulled from my body, and they come to rest against my lips at the same time as Jensen's cock nudges my opening. He glides his glistening fingers into my mouth, urging me to lick him clean as he thrusts his hips upwards into my heat. It's been minutes since I finished him, swallowed every last drop of his cum, yet he is already rock hard for me.

It's a dizzying feeling, being able to feel the desire he has for me. It spurs me on, activates my devilish side. I once thought Jensen West was the devil, and if that is true, then dammit, I want to be his Lilith.

Still lapping at his fingers deep inside my mouth, I begin to move my hips, small figure-eights turning into languid back-and-forth movements. With each upward thrust of Jensen's hips, I slam my own movement down with just enough caution to ensure I'm not crushing him under my weight.

He can tell I'm holding back, and it doesn't make him happy.

"Eleanor!" he barks my name, reaching up with his other hand to slap me across my breast–not Princess, not love. "Fuck me like you mean it. Stop holding back!"

Fingers leave my mouth, both of his hands coming down to grab my hips. Not hold, not grip–he *grabs* them. Jensen wraps his fingers around my hips with punishing force, using nothing but his arms to lift me up further and pull me down harder on top of him with each thrust of our bodies. "I said I want you to fuck me like you mean it, goddammit!"

And between his fingers digging into me almost painfully, the constant give and take of our motions, and the pure desire for this man, a tidal wave of feeling soon overtakes my body.

My toes curl into the sheets that have bunched around us, my back arching towards the heavens as my hair tickles his legs beneath me. My breasts bounce almost to the point of pain, and sweat trickles down my spine. And just when I think it can't get any better, that I have already died and gone to heaven, Jensen releases one hand from my hip, bringing it between our bodies, and rubs my clit as I tumble wave over wave and crash into oblivion.

Jensen pulls me into his chest and rolls me over, tucking me into his side. That's how we stay tangled together for hours upon hours. We lay in bed early into the morning–touching, caressing, fucking, talking.

And without certainty, I know, in this moment, that this time, I couldn't run from Jensen West.

Even if I wanted to.

SAN DIEGO SOL TO TAKE ON ORLANDO BEFORE INTERNATIONAL BREAK.

Soccer Daily Online: For Immediate Release

A welcomed break comes to much of the team after a grueling two-week travel schedule concludes.

San Diego, CA, July 11- With the World Cup being just over one year away, international teams will be converging around the world as many players travel to their home countries for training. The team will break after their match against Orlando this Saturday.

Coach James Calder is quoted as saying, "While several of our key players will be training with their international clubs over the next two weeks, we look forward to continuing to work with our players who will be staying with us in San Diego. Our hard work and perseverance throughout the season is not something we take lightly, and we will continue that dedication during this international break."

END RELEASE

You know that feeling when you check on your clothes in the dryer, only to find that they're half-dry and disgustingly warm? Next, imagine taking those clothes out of the dryer and putting them onto your body while they are still damp, clinging to your skin like a parasite. Now, wearing those clothes, go walk around outside in the middle of the summer.

If you can complete that task without passing out from heat stroke, you'll come close to knowing what it currently feels like to be in Orlando.

Truly, the person who decided it was a smart idea to schedule an away game at three o'clock in the afternoon in July in what is known as the Sunshine State should be fired. Or at least be forced to live in this hell-hole of a human furnace for the rest of their life.

I just keep reminding myself that after today's game, I have two glorious weeks off while many players from around the world are playing with their respective countries. Unique to soccer, international break occurs a few times each season and is when international players from around the world travel to their home countries to play with their national teams. It can be for training camps, exhibition games, and even tournaments with money and trophies on the line.

In years past, it would have gutted me that I wasn't chosen to return to England to play for the national team. My anger would have gotten the best of me, and I would have blamed it on anyone and everyone except for myself. The truth is simply that I'm getting older, and there are a hell of a lot of talented young blokes coming up through the ranks.

This year, I'm also looking forward to almost two full weeks of uninterrupted time with Eleanor–starting with tonight when I whisk her away from the team and surprise her with three days at Disney World.

It took some finagling on my part, but I was finally able to convince Coach to let us both fly back to California later this week–on my dime of course, after we spend a few days at the Florida theme park. Not that I mind spending money on her. Hell, I love to lavash her with surprise gifts, and I've already been dreaming of the off season when we can actually travel to some of the many places we've talked about during our late-night cuddle sessions.

Yeah, Jensen West has turned into a cuddler. Can you fucking believe that shit?

I surely couldn't at first, but honestly, Eleanor is like a fucking drug to me, and I'll never stop looking for my next fix.

Initially, we tried to keep our relationship quiet around the locker room. While I knew from my previous recognizance that there were no rules against a coach and player having a relationship, Eleanor still worried that she would be perceived differently by the rest of the coaching staff and players.

That didn't last.

Or, it would have if two of my teammates didn't walk in on us while I had Eleanor spread out over the massage table in the therapist's room, ass in the air, her panties shoved in her mouth to keep her quiet as she came on my cock.

Needless to say, news spread quickly after that little stunt.

And we've been much more discrete since, always double-and triple-checking that doors are locked before partaking in any extracurricular activities while on the clock.

Besides, the only worse thing than being called into the principal's office is when that principal is your girlfriend's dad. Or, in my case, just swap out principal with boss. That conversation with Big Man Bigsby certainly did *not* go well.

He threatened to boot me from the team, to send me back to England, to have my name blacklisted from anything having to do with soccer, and even said he would send Eleanor to work across the country, making sure I'd never be able to touch his "little girl" again.

I was two seconds away from telling Maxwell Bigsby that I'm the only man his little girl calls Daddy now, but was saved when Eleanor intervened, telling her father how much she is learning from me, enjoying spending time with me, and that she is an adult now who is free to make her own decisions.

Then, last week after an intimate dinner at an up-and-coming restaurant in San Diego, a photographer snagged a pic of us as we left the restaurant. The following morning, the picture appeared on several celebrity gossip sites with questions swirling around *Jensen West's Mystery Woman*.

Being a celebrity is brutal. It's something I am used to from many years as a professional athlete. And while Eleanor and I spoke at length about the territory that came along with dating me in public, I know it crushed her to see the headlines that were written about her.

Jensen West and his Hungry Hungry Hippo.

Jensen, Mystery Woman, and Baby Makes Three?

When those headlines appeared, I was seeing red all day, ready to row with anyone who even breathed in my direction incorrectly.

Needless to say, it's been a fucking rollercoaster of the last few months, and both she and I need and deserve this time alone with one another.

But first, I have to get through this game.

Orlando is known to have one of the toughest playing atmospheres in the league. From their scrappy style of play to their extremely loud supporters, they cause a ruckus both on the pitch and in the stands for every opponent who comes into their stadium. And today is no different.

Their drumline is in full force, leading chants that echo around the stadium. Flags are being waved throughout the section of the stadium reserved for designated supporter groups, and a raucous noise erupts from around the building when rain begins to pour down from the heavens in heavy sheets only seventeen minutes into the match.

The energy is fantastic, the rain feels absolutely sublime against my body as it muddles with the salty sweat clinging to my skin, and while I'm anxious to finish the match and start my two weeks of bliss, my head is firmly focused on the game before me.

In the thirty-fifth minute, we're up over the home team two-to-one, and I'm feeling confident as we near the halfway mark of the match. The guys are connecting passes, constantly pressing upfield, and Schmidt has had a few killer saves that will certainly make him a contender for Save Of The Week in the highlight reels.

A late tackle to the back of my leg from their centerback takes me down hard, just inside the box. The ref immediately holds a yellow card in the air before awarding me a well-deserved penalty kick.

Their fans are going absolute bonkers, screaming and yelling at the ref for awarding our team a chance to widen our lead even further. A few plastic cups make their way onto the field, but I don't let it get to me. Instead I focus on my team, quickly talking through the strategy we've practiced time and time again during training.

And then, I step up to the ball–just me and the opposing team's keeper. I inhale once, filling my lungs with fresh air, then exhale, wiping the rain from my eyes as I take the few steps to my mark.

I run to the ball, my eyes laser-focused on the top right corner of the net. And as my foot connects with the ball and the keeper leaves his line, the ball soars up, up, up, before curving to the left, landing squarely in the back of the net.

The crowd erupts in a chorus of boos, more debris careens onto the pitch, and as the fans around us scream obscenities at our team, I can't help but turn to find Eleanor on the sidelines, where I quickly shoot her a sly wink before turning back to my team on the field.

Then, in the blink of an eye, it all goes to shit.

A group of children in the first few rows begin chanting, and what I initially think is a chorus of "honk, honk, honk" quickly becomes a clear, ongoing cadence of "oink, oink, oink." Bad enough that this absolute disgrace started from children, some as young as six, but all too soon, it spreads through the adults in the sections around them, too. Adult men, calling out disgusting words about Eleanor–about *my* Eleanor–as women around them laugh and egg on their taunting.

Silently, I'm praying she is far enough way, that she can't hear the hurtful words that are being hurled toward the relationship I share with her, but with one look at her face, silent tears falling from her beautiful, green eyes and mixing with the rain coming down around her, I can tell she has heard every fucking word.

Something inside me snaps. My vision blurs, shutting out the faces of every person in the stadium. The only person I can see is the man directly in front of me–Orlando's goal keeper–and the son-of-a-bitch is *laughing*–standing between the two posts of the net, clapping his oversized gloved hands, and laughing like a fucking fool.

Laugh at me all you want. Make fun of my upbringing, or my often out-of-control lifestyle, or how I play the game all you fucking want. But to bring Eleanor into this?

Abso-fucking-lutely not.

I fucking *rage.*

Cole notices a second too late, his hand coming to wrap around my bicep. But I'm faster and easily shake him off. I take one, two, three steps toward the keeper, shoving him with both hands. While not expecting it, he's slightly knocked off balance but quickly recovers. Still, I'm faster, and this time, my fist connects with the side of his face before he tumbles to the turf beneath our feet.

It takes Cole as well as two other guys to pull me off him, and within seconds of us being pulled apart, I'm being shown a red card and being directed to leave the pitch.

"Making fun of fucking women?!" I shout as I walk away. "How fucking dare you!"

I'm slow to make my way off the field, not caring about the fines I'll be racking up for my behavior. I make my way down the side of the pitch, stopping near the coaches and technical staff. I bypass Coach, knowing already what I have coming to me from him, and stop directly in front of Eleanor.

I shouldn't do it–not here, not in front of these people who have no clue what a treasure this woman is–but I can't stop myself from reaching out and cupping her face in my hand. "I deserve whatever is coming to me due to that outburst, but you, Love? You do not deserve one fucking ounce of disrespect that just happened. You are worth *so* much more than any of those assholes."

Expecting to see sadness or trepidation in her gaze, I'm shocked when I meet her eyes and see anger. Toward me?

Toward the people in the stadium? I'm not sure yet, but I have a feeling I'm going to find out soon.

I keep walking to the player's tunnel, aware that the halftime whistle will be blowing in just a few minutes. And before I disappear into the locker room, I take one look behind me, raise my middle finger in the air, and yell, "Fuck you, Orlando," as loud as I can.

SAN DIEGO SOL RECEIVES RED CARD AGAINST ORLANDO

Soccer Daily Online: For Immediate Release

Despite the red card, San Diego remains ahead at the half.

San Diego, CA, July 14- Soccer's bad boy is back with a vengeance! After scoring off a penalty kick, the star athlete attacked the opposing team's goalkeeper after fans of Orlando verbally attacked West's supposed girlfriend and conditioning coach, Eleanor Bigsby.

Coach James Calder declined to comment.

END RELEASE

ELEANOR

12.

THE ABSOLUTE IRE coursing through my body right now is enough to fuel an entire city. I'm upset about what the crowd was chanting, clearly a taunt made about me to get under Jensen's skin, and it worked. That's not what I'm pissed about though.

No. I'm purely livid over Jensen's complete lack of respect for his team, for his coaches–hell, even for me.

He is fiercely protective of me, and he's shown that time and time again. He's shown that protectiveness and loyalty when he tried to shield me from the public when we first began dating. He demonstrated it by hiding every tabloid he could find when we ended up on the cover, even in the way he stood up to my father after our little afternoon massage table mishap.

But that anger he showed on the field, the way he attacked the opposing team's player out of pure rage...it has no place anywhere near me.

I'm a few minutes behind him when I head into the locker room at half time along with the team and coaching staff. And while I want to have more than a word with him, I know Coach will be first in line to tear him a new asshole.

I'm not even in the door when I hear him, ranting and raving, his English accent more pronounced than usual. "Utter. Fucking. Bollocks!"

Metal slams in the distance and a chair comes crashing through the room.

"That's ENOUGH!" a voice–Coach–booms through the locker room, quieting the storm to near-deafening silence.

Looking at his coaching counterpart, he barks several instructions before locking eyes with me. "You–with me."

Heat flashes across my skin, creeping up my cheeks until I feel as hot as a microwaved pizza roll that splattered from the confines of its toasty shell. I follow Coach James into a smaller room adjacent to the main locker room, my head hung in defeat. How the hell am I going to take the blame for this shit when I had nothing to do with it?

I crumble into a chair opposite Coach, ready to drop my hands into my head, but he speaks, leaving me near speechless before I have the chance.

"Elle, I know I was not on board with your employment when you first started this year, and I am still not completely on board with you having...relations...with a member of the team. That aside, what happened on that pitch today had absolutely nothing to do with you and everything to do with the atmosphere of the game. People will do whatever they can to get a rise out of their opponent. I am simply, truly sorry that today, it came at your expense. You have been an asset to our club, and I will protect you in any way possible. I'm not sure exactly what it is that you have done to that man, but up until today, he truly seems to be in a better headspace than I have seen him in quite some time."

I can't help but give him a weak smile.

"I know this is asking more than your outlined job duties, but I would appreciate it if you tried to speak with him before we have to return to the pitch."

He rises, and I give him a short nod, telling him without words that I will oblige his request. "I'll send him in. And again, I cannot express how truly sorry I am."

Waiting for Jensen, I play over the events of the last twenty minutes. And when the anger starts to rise again, and I realize that the anger isn't because of what was said about me, but what Jensen did to the team, it truly hits me for the first time that just maybe, I am starting to be part of the Sol family and that perhaps, soccer isn't as bad of a sport as I initially thought.

The door opens, but I don't raise my eyes until I hear the quiet *snick* of the door signifying that it's just he and I in the room–away from listening ears.

When our eyes meet, the rage in mine is met by a mix of sadness and disgust in Jensen's. He looks tormented, like he's aged ten years in the past twenty minutes. An absolute wreck of a man stands before me.

As I rise from my chair, he tugs my wrist until I'm wrapped in his arms. Momentarily blinded by the feel of his body, I quickly gain control of my emotions, pushing him away.

"Don't!" I snap out.

He looks physically pained as he stares back at me. "Love, I'm so sorry. I just–" his hands come up to tug on his short strands, "I lost control. I heard what they were saying, and it was too much. Shit like that should never be said about any woman, but especially you. Eleanor, you're everything good and pure about this world. You're so fucking wonderful and gorgeous. Love, you're simply *gorgeous...*"

"Jensen, stop." I place my hand on his forearm, trying to ground him, to bring him back to the here and now. "Listen, you fucked up big time out there. But you shouldn't be in here apologizing to me. You should be out there, apologizing to your *team*. Because they're the ones you let down today. I will always appreciate you sticking up for me and will always want you on my side, but today, you let a bunch of childish assholes dictate your attitude, and that might affect the outcome of this game for your entire team. Let me worry about what people are saying about me. You worry about doing your job."

He pulls me into another hug, and this time, I let him. His hands rub up and down my arms. "I'm so fucking sorry, Love. So fucking sorry."

"Go apologize to the guys before they head back out. I'll be back as soon as the match is over."

Just about forty-five minutes later, we're back in the locker room. The guys did their best to hold on to their lead but ended up in a draw, each team taking a point from the tie. I'm still slightly aggravated with Jensen and still slightly hurt at the horrible words that were slung my way, but above all, I'm proud of the team for being able to end up playing an entire half, down a man, and still end up tying.

For the first time this season, I sneak into the press room where post-game interviews are being held. Coach is up first.

"Issues aside, and I know there were quite a few issues with this match, I am proud of how the boys held their own out there. I would be amiss if I didn't at least briefly touch on what led to our red card today, and I would like to go on record by saying that I do not condone the behavior exhibited by Jensen today. However, I also do not condone the complete disrespect towards a member of my coaching staff by members of the home team's fan base. The blatant mockery made of Elle Bigsby should not be tolerated by any team within our league or at any sporting event around the world."

Jensen is asked to speak next, and he somewhat hesitantly takes his place at the conference table amongst the microphones and phones waiting to record each and every word. "First, I would like to apologize to Orlando's keeper for the shiner I've surely left him with during today's match." A few low chuckles come from around the crowded room.

"Next, to my team, I truly apologize for letting you down today. I let the situation in the stands get the best of me, and I one-hundred percent believe that cost us the win. I'm nowhere near perfect–hell, you all know that, but the anger I showed today was the absolute worst side of me and is a side I regret showing to the world. Lastly, To Eleanor, I apologize for not allowing you to stand up for yourself and for taking that option away from you when I acted out of turn on the pitch."

He looks around the throngs of people until he finds me, his eyes locking on mine. "Truly, I cannot put into words just how sorry I am."

Jensen pushes back from the table and stands before making his way back to the first row of seats among his players.

I'm halfway out of the room when a deep voice from a male reporter calls my name. "Elle, would you give us a statement?"

Slowly, I turn around, slightly embarrassed about being put on the spot. I look to Coach James who gives me a nod, signaling me to approach the table if I'd like.

And I do, my feet moving of their own accord. I'm not sure what I'm planning to say, even as I take a seat before the numerous reporters. But once I sit down and clear my throat, the words just start, the nerves evident by the tremble in my voice as I speak. "Um...it's a unique situation that finds me in front of you today. I'm certainly not the first woman to find herself in what is essentially known as an all-boys club, and I know I won't be the last. My team, my club," I look around the room at the coaches and players, my crazy little found family, "they have treated me with nothing but respect since day one, and I'm only saddened that I was not afforded the same respect from the fans of Orlando today that I am given by my club every single day. As one of the few women in the industry, I see on a daily basis how damning women can be to one another and how damaging the effects can be to a woman's self-esteem. It's sad to see women in the stands perpetuating that hateful narrative, sickening to see men join in on taunting unrelated to the game in any sort of way, and horrible to see that what started the entire situation was a group of children. I only hope that, as a species, we can do better in the future to keep banter focused on what is happening on the field and to stop hateful rhetoric surrounding someone's appearance. That could be any of our daughters in the future. It could be your sister or your best friend. And if it is something you wouldn't say to any of them, perhaps in the future, you'll think twice before saying it about a total stranger. Thank you."

I stand and walk from the room, head held high as the room sits in silence.

Back in the locker room, I'm finishing a few training notes when the guys file into the room. One by one, my team enters while clapping, some offering me pats on the back while others pull me into big bear hugs while speaking words of encouragement into my ears. It feels good to know that these men have my back. It feels really good.

And when Jensen enters the room behind everyone else and scoops me into his arms in front of everyone, I know this is where I am truly meant to be.

I might have gone into this situation counting down the days until my last day with San Diego Sol, but now, I'm simply praying they don't go by too quickly.

Jensen sets me down on the floor, almost dragging me behind him to the small room we sat in together less than an hour ago. "Are you still mad at me, Love?"

I reach up to brush a few stray strands of hair off his forehead that had escaped his post-shower styling. "I was never mad–just upset over the situation as a whole. I want the ability to hold my own, to stick up for myself. I love being part of a team with you, but sometimes, you need to let me find my own way. And it's okay if I stumble a few times along that path. I know you'll be there to catch me if I do."

He tilts my chin upward, bending over to place a chaste kiss on my lips. "I don't know what I ever did to deserve you, Eleanor, but I truly am the luckiest fucking bastard on the planet."

I give a little laugh, kissing him again.

"I do have one more thing that may help to make up for it," he says, a sly grin spreading across his face.

"Tell me it's first-class tickets back home, and I may just forgive you in advance for any future mistakes you make in advance," I joke.

"How about I do you one better?"

"What's better than first class?"

He brings my hand to his lips, placing a kiss on each of my knuckles. "Well, you are my Princess, and there is a pretty big castle right up the road. How about a few days with me at the Most Magical Place on Earth before we take a chartered flight back to California?"

My eyes go wide, my mouth dropping while I stand there in stunned silence.

"Hell, say something, Love."

"I...I love it! I've always dreamed of going, but I've only ever been to Disneyland! Are you seriously taking me? What about the team? What about clothes?" My mind speeds along, going a mile a minute. I'm in full-on do-not-pass-go do-not-collect-two-hundred-dollars as my brain tries to comprehend how he pulled this surprise off.

"I had to pull a few strings, but yes, we're seriously going. In fact, we're leaving from here in ten minutes, and we have a private car transporting us to our hotel. The team is flying back tonight, and I had some help in gathering a few of your belongings before we left. Anything else–well, we'll just buy it."

I'm absolutely floored that he planned such an elaborate surprise for us, our first weekend away together. And at Disney of all places! I may be twenty-two, but I'll be damned if I'm not a princess at heart.

Turkey legs and churros, here I come!

SOCCER STUD WEST CAUGHT IN PUBLIC WITH HIS VERY OWN PRINCESS

Gossip Nation Online: For Immediate Release

After an upset caused by West in Orlando, the bad boy steps out in public with conditioning coach, Eleanor Bigsby.

San Diego, CA, July 16- Confirming their rumored relationship with a trip to Disney World, the pair was seen cozying up to one another on the teacups. Sharing more than theme park popcorn, the duo was also seen sharing intimate moments and stolen glances as they chatted with fans throughout the parks.

Neither party could be reached for immediate comment.

END RELEASE

In the last three days, I've nearly thrown up on those God-awful teacups, eaten my weight in mouse-shaped waffles, and sang that wretched song about a small world approximately one-thousand-nine-hundred-and-eighty-three times. More miles have been walked each day than I normally put on during a game, and I am now the proud owner of not one but *three* pairs of mouse ears. Yet still, it was one of the best experiences of my life, and I would do it all over again simply to see the look of pure elation on Eleanor's face as we experienced each new hidden nook and cranny the parks had to offer.

Being a professional athlete has always had its perks. I never have to wait for a reservation at any of the swankiest restaurants, things almost always go my way, and I've even been able to use my status to skirt the law a time or two–a fact I'm not incredibly proud of but not too unassuming to admit. However, the same job that has brought me privilege for much of my life can also lead to a life in the public eye. While soccer is still not as popular in the states as it is across the rest of the world, I am still recognized on a fairly regular basis. Luckily, it only happened a few times while we were on holiday, and every interaction was positive–something that hasn't always been true of the past.

Initially, I was worried each time someone approached, anxious that each interaction would be fraught with negative attention not toward me, but toward the woman whose hand stayed firmly grasped in mine as we traipsed the world of make-believe we had entered.

But it was just the opposite. As I casually chatted with fans of the sport, never turning down an autograph or request for a selfie, Eleanor stood by my side, offering to take the pictures for whoever was brave enough to approach us. She made fast friends with everyone with her carefree attitude and penchant for not taking anything too seriously. Several times throughout our stay, she too even jumped in pictures with people, swapped Instagram handles with a few, and even exchanged phone numbers with a girl a few years younger than herself who was hoping to also work for a professional sports team after graduation.

The entire trip, she had an absolutely infectious smile plastered to her face, but none as much as last night–our last full night. We spent the day at Magic Kingdom, where she met and took pictures with a princess who had hair as fiery red and wild as her own. They shared hugs and laughs, as I'm learning Eleanor does with almost everyone she meets, before I surprised her with an early dinner inside the castle.

To end the night, we stopped at the candy store and filled up bags with chocolates, fudge, candy floss, and many other assortments from the shop. Then, we retired to our room—a quaint little bungalow on the water at one of the best hotels with views of the castle where we had previously eaten. I positioned her in a chair in front of the floor to ceiling window, and with synchronized music floating throughout the villa, I emptied a packet of popping candy into my mouth, knelt before her, and devoured her cunt like a feast, listening to her chant my name over and over again as she came on my tongue. The sounds and sights of fireworks bursting in the night sky were our backdrop, and the candy-coated rocks exploded against my tongue along with the sweet taste of Eleanor's release.

Moving beside me on the crisp, white hotel linens, Eleanor stretches, her alabaster, naked skin bathed in the fresh light of day pouring in through the windows. Her hair is even more tousled than normal due to hours of late-night fucking, and her toes are cold as she presses them to my calves, squirming impossibly closer to me in the bed.

"Do we *have* to leave today?" she pouts, and it's adorable in a stupidly cute way–like a fluffy, new puppy is when begging for a treat.

Pulling her body flush with mine, I run my hands up and down her smooth, cool skin before brushing a kiss over her lips. Morning breath be damned. I'm so enamored with the woman that she could skip brushing her teeth for a month, and I'd still want to kiss her every damn day.

"Aye, Love, we do." I bring one of her hands to my lips, pressing a kiss against each finger. "But what if I promise to bring you back after the season is finished?"

She beams up at me, her magnificent, slightly-crooked smile not only making her seem younger than she is, but also making her endearing to anyone who is lucky enough to see her. I must look to her in return with a stupidly silly look on my face because she quickly calls me out. "What's that face for?"

"Just wondering what a cynical old fuck like myself did to wind up with such a sexy young thing like you."

Her laugh fills the room, and when I grab her sides, tickling her in retaliation, she squeals before pulling away. It's cute that she thinks she can escape me. I pull her back into me before holding her down on the bed, one large palm spread out over her chest. All of her squirming and squealing has me hard as a fucking rock, and I make sure she's aware of that fact, grinding myself into the soft flesh of her pelvis. "I want you one more time before we have to leave."

She lifts her hips off the mattress in a silent response, and there is no doubt in my mind that I want to wake up next to this woman every single day.

The woman truly is a creature unto herself–so pliant and malleable, so open to trying anything and everything new, and so damn responsive. I can make her wet with just my words, ravenous with a simple stare, and command her body with my own. I've had multiple women at once, simultaneously shared partners with my best friend, yet still, I'd choose Eleanor over any of those other experiences every fucking time. People might say the land of make-believe we've been in the last few days is magical, but it doesn't come close to the magic that seeps from every pore of this woman's body.

I palm her breasts, loving the way they feel under my hands, before I roll her nipples between my fingers, increasing pressure until she's gasping and keening, asking for more from me–demanding more of me.

Removing my hands from her tits, as painful as it is, I place one on her leg, knowing the faster I move her into position, the faster I can sink inside her soft, wet cunt. "Turn over, Princess. I want to fuck you from behind, want to grab that pretty hair of yours, and watch your ass slam back against me as I enter you with each thrust."

"God, yes," she purrs, moving her leg from between us to flip herself over.

And I'm so fucking hard and so turned on by watching her body move beneath me that I don't even notice until it's too late that her foot is close to my head...way too close to my head... until it kicks me in the side of the face...hard.

Her words come flying out, an apology almost as garbled as my head feels. "Oh, my God, Jensen, I am so sorry! Please, please, please forgive me! Fuck! Jesus fuck, are you okay?"

It takes a few seconds for the stars behind my eyes to dissipate, but when they do, I can't help but start laughing. And once it starts, it doesn't stop. I'm roaring, my entire body shaking in a fit of laughter. My stomach hurts, I can barely catch my breath, and I have tears trailing down my cheeks.

What seems like ages later, she must sense that I'm okay, and she rolls her lips over her teeth, trying to stifle her own giggles.

One of the best types of laughter, when you laugh until your abs hurt and when you finally stop, you look at each other only to burst again–that's the laughter we're sharing right now. Each time we stop, it quickly starts up again, only to be peppered with *I'm sorrys* from Eleanor and *I'm okays* from me.

Finally, we calm down enough to speak in full sentences, both of us with tear-streaked faces from laughing until we cried. I can't remember the last time I had this much fun with another person, can't remember the last time I was so utterly smitten by a woman. Probably never.

"Christ, woman, never thought I'd have to enter concussion protocol due to a sex mishap."

She sits up, grabbing my hand. "I'm so sorry, Jensen. Are you sure you're okay?"

Pulling her toward me until she is straddling my lap, I cup her face in my hands, staring earnestly into her eyes. "I promise. And hell, sex is supposed to be fun. I don't think either of us can deny that what just happened was funny as hell."

Eleanor kisses me, a deep, sloppy kiss where she licks into my mouth. "I really thought I hurt you."

Despite the laughter and our impromptu injury time out, I'm still painfully hard. "Nah, Princess, didn't even put a dent in my dick." I thrust up to her, my length pressing between us.

Her hips wiggle against me, creating a delicious friction that is enough to make my mouth salivate. "I guess I better take care of that, shouldn't I?" She moves once, placing my cock at the entrance of her pussy before sliding down, impaling herself with my length in one fluid movement. "Just let me stay on top this time. We need you to be healthy for when the season resumes."

I'd laugh if the movement didn't feel so fucking decadent, her cunt slowly sliding up and down my shaft as her tits bounce up and down, the tight little buds of her nipples teasing against my chest. "Baby, you can kick me in the head every fucking day if this is how you're going to make up for it."

Her hands come up to wrap around my neck, fingers lightly scraping up and down my scalp. I reciprocate the action, tangling my own fingers into her hair before tugging her head backward, giving me access to the column of her neck. Licking up the exposed skin, I revel in the tang of her skin, a mixture of salt and something sweet enough it would put the nectar of the Gods to shame. "I'm fucking enamored by you, Eleanor. I want to be your everything, baby."

A low moan escapes her as her hands fall from my head, nails dragging down my back as she scrapes and claws. "You already are," she pants, continuing to assault my body with the dichotomy of the slight pain of her nails and absolute bliss of her pussy wrapped around my dick.

I'm feral, in an absolute frenzy of lust over her confession, and in need of having her as close as possible.

"Fuck me, Jensen!" she gasps into the air. "Fuck me and show me that I'm yours in every sense of the way."

Christ, I think I love this woman.

I hold her close, our chests flush against each other. We're so close, a human hair wouldn't fit between us, and it's the most surreal moment in the world. Our bodies move as one, me pistoning my hips over and over and over again as she slams her hips in time with my movements.

It's rough, and dirty, and messy, and so uniquely us, but at the same time, something *is* different. It's different because while we're still connecting, still fucking, but this time, we're not *just* fucking–we're making love.

And I already can't wait to do it again.

SAN DIEGO SOL'S COACH, ELEANOR BIGSBY, TO APPEAR IN SPORTS MONTHLY

Gossip Nation Online: For Immediate Release

Quickly becoming a household name, Coach Eleanor Bigsby will appear in her first photo shoot for the magazine.

San Diego, CA, July 30- After facing both criticism and praise following the incident in Orlando earlier this month, Eleanor will bare more than her "Sol" in an upcoming issue of the popular sports periodical.

Coach Eleanor Bigsby was quoted as saying, "It is important for all women to learn to embrace themselves, much the way I have learned to embrace my own strengths and flaws. The time is now to be strong role models for future generations of young girls, and loving ourselves is the ultimate way to set that precedent."

END RELEASE

Two weeks without the full team had flown by, and while I was still at the stadium each day, it had been much more relaxed. I actually had time to sit at my small desk each day, tracking notes and players' progress. I spent time pouring over session notes, plotting progress, and spending one-on-one time with the players that hadn't traveled to be with their international clubs–Jensen included.

Since returning from Florida, I'd spent more nights at his house than at my own apartment. We fell into a quick routine, sharing breakfast in the morning before coming to training in the same car, working together in the afternoons, and then returning to his house where we made dinner each night before tumbling between the sheets together in a mess of limbs and passion.

The man fucks me like a beast. More often than not, he is rough, pulling my hair, slapping my ass, and leaving marks on my skin. I relish in his attention, loving the way he makes me feel physically and mentally.

But even more than the sex–and trust me, there is a *lot* of sex–is how much he makes me laugh, how much he pampers me, trusts me with stories about his past, and how much he has helped me learn about what I had been thrown into at the beginning of the season.

My phone vibrating across my tiny desk snaps me back to the present. I had been daydreaming for so long that the screen-saver bounced across my computer screen, a soccer ball tumbling around, always searching for the net but never quite hitting its mark.

Ophelia: *CHECK YOUR WORK EMAIL!*
Ophelia: *I'm coming down there!*
Ophelia: *This is HUGE!*

Thanks to her job in the marketing department, Ophelia is often in the know of up-and-coming gossip before the rest of us are. Even better, she has a solid handle on what is just that–gossip–versus what had actual truth behind it.

Moving the mouse of the computer, I wake up my monitor, clicking on my emails. Three new messages blink at me, and taking a quick look at the subject lines, I choose the odd one out–an email from the Director of Marketing.

To: E.Bigsby@Sol.Com
From: R.Green@Sol.com
Subject: Potential Collaboration Opportunity
Good afternoon, Eleanor,

I'm reaching out to you with a unique opportunity that I am hoping you will consider. Earlier today, a member of *Sports Monthly* contacted the team. It seems that you have made quite an impression on the women who work behind the scenes at the magazine after the video of the incident, which occured in Orlando, hit the internet.

The magazine is currently looking for models for their upcoming annual *Bare It All* issue and would like to feature you in the spread. If you are unfamiliar with the magazine and this issue, it has historically featured notable and up-and-coming-athletes wearing nothing but a few strategically placed items related to their sport.

I understand that this is outside of the normal scope of your job. However, in my professional opinion, I do believe that this could not only open new avenues for you within the professional sporting industry, but is also an important way to further the narrative that bodies of all sizes are beautiful, strong, and belong in the field of athletics.

Should you wish to further discuss this opportunity, please do not hesitate to reach out.

While a decision must be made by the end of this week, I do not want you to rush into this; however, I do hope that you will seriously consider what the magazine is offering.

I look forward to hearing from you,

Rochelle Green

On my third read through of the email, my mind spinning as I try to grasp what Rochelle had written, the small, blonde tornado that is Ophelia twirls into my small office, leaving a trail of dust in her path.

She doesn't bother with greetings or pleasantries, opting to all but screech loud enough that I'm sure they hear her on the other side of the country. "You're going to be in *Sports Monthly!*"

My eyes bounce back and forth between my computer screen and my friend. I'm unable to string words together, fairly certain that I'm in a state of mild shock.

While I haven't followed much of what has been said in the media after what Ophelia calls *The Orlando Experience*, almost all of what I have seen was overwhelmingly positive. Women in the sports and entertainment industry rallied behind me, sharing stories of their own experiences with body shaming. Several teams of various sports stepped up to release their own anti-harassment policies, and the Sol has been on my side the entire time.

My father didn't contact me until I was back in San Diego,

but when I returned, he was the first person who called me. Along with heartfelt apologies, he offered to do whatever he could to make me feel at ease with continuing to work for the team. He offered counseling to me, asked if I thought the team needed sensitivity training, and even offered to speak to the league on my behalf about the incident.

And while I appreciated how protective he was being of me, I declined his offerings, assuring him that it was nothing the team or league could have prevented. This was about a bunch of rogue soccer fans who took things too far.

"Elle, you're going to do it, right? *Please* tell me you're going to say yes! This is huge–one of the biggest selling magazine issues every year across all print media–and they want your gorgeous body on its pages!"

Dazed, I finally settle my gaze on Ophelia. "I...I have no idea. To say I'm overwhelmed is an understatement."

Finding a nearby chair at one of the vacant desks, she pulls it up across my desk and plops into the chair without grace. Unlike the charm and poise she turns on when the guys are around, when it's just her and I, she's a total slouch. I think it's part of the reason we get along so well. Rarely do I put extra fuss into my appearance or how others perceive me, so when she lets that guard down, it's like catching a glimpse at the true woman she is.

"Tell me why you're hesitant to do it, Elle. Spill it all, and let's figure it out because when I tell you this is a huge deal, I mean that this is a huge deal. Some of the biggest athletes in the world have been featured in this issue–not just from soccer, but from all sports. And I don't think there has ever been a condi-tioning coach featured, let alone a woman from a team's coaching staff."

I sit back in my chair, cocking my neck back to look up at the white, drop-tiled ceiling panels. "That's just the thing. Why would they want me? I'm a nobody, a small-time coach in a huge, professional organization. They'd be better putting Jensen or Cole in the magazine. Hell, even Coach James would rock it."

"But they don't want the men; they want *you*. You stood up to the haters when you took part in that press conference. You showed you wouldn't tolerate the hate thrown your way and that you are better than anyone who speaks like that. You've shown that you're a woman who stands up for other women and that feminism can be sexy as hell."

"As rare as it is for me to say this, I think I need to talk to my dad." Picking up the headset on my desk phone, I dial his extension, surprised when he picks up on the second ring. We don't keep tabs on each other as closely as some families do, so I wasn't even sure he would be in the state of California, let alone his office.

His booming voice cuts through the silence of the room as Ophelia looks at me across the desk, wide eyes looking for any breadcrumb of a clue as to what my answer will be.

It comes as no surprise that my dad already knows about the offer from *Sports Monthly*, but it does come as a surprise that he tells me the ultimate decision is up to me.

"Of course, I have some reservations about the entire thing, Honey." I can't remember the last time he called me by a term of endearment. I find it tugs at my heart. "But that doesn't come from a place of you posing stark naked in a magazine, it comes from a place of wanting to make sure you are protected–always. It comes from a place where you will always be the five-year-old little girl that came into my life and became part of my family."

Well, shit. I wasn't planning on getting emotional today, but here I am.

Hanging up with my dad, I feel more confident in making a decision.

"I think I'm going to do it."

Ophelia squeals with delight, jumping up from her chair and dancing around the office.

"Going to do what, Love?" Jensen and Cole choose that minute to walk into the office, freshly showered and dressed after working on the field through the afternoon. My heart still flutters every time he calls me Love, and while I know we're nowhere near that step in our early relationship, I long for the day when he says those words to me in another capacity. He walks behind my desk, dropping a quick kiss on the crown of my head.

Still jumping around, in sky-high heels she wears almost daily, I'm afraid Ophelia is going to roll an ankle as she picks right back up with an infectious good mood. "Please let me tell them–please, please please! I need to live vicariously through you, Elle!"

I hold up one finger to her, motioning for her to pause. "First, let me just say that I haven't one hundred percent made up my mind yet."

Gesturing to Ophelia, I give her the green light to continue. She perches on the side of my desk, crossing her legs daintily over one another, back to the prim and proper facade she plasters on in front of the athletes. When I first met her, I thought it was because she wanted to show off an air of importance in front of them. As I've grown to know her, I've learned that it is actually insecurity that plagues her, which makes her act the way she does.

"Well..." she stretches out the word for dramatic effect, "our little fiery redhead behind the desk over there was propositioned by *Sports Monthly* today. They've apparently been keeping tabs on her since *The Orlando Experience* and want to feature her in the *Bare it All* issue because she's an awesome feminist who is fighting for equality throughout our industry."

Ophelia squeals again, doing a little shimmy from her perch

on my desk, Cole looks on impassively, and Jensen absolutely beams with a rakish smile that causes something other than my heart to flutter this time.

"That's fucking brilliant!" He pulls me up from my chair, lifting me up until my toes only skate the floor beneath me before giving me a little twirl in the small space between my chair and desk. Setting me back down on the ground, he tucks a forever errant curl behind my ear. "Seriously, Eleanor, that's a big fucking deal. To do that after *The Orlando Experience*," he throws air quotes around it as he says it, "shows to everyone that you mean fucking business and that you're not afraid of being exactly who you are. It's standing up for every woman who has ever been called something less than kind. Hell, the only time my dick was in the news was because of an ex who leaked photos of me. I had no say in that. And let's face it, I have a banging body, but I'd prefer to be in charge of who sees it and when."

My mind reels with what Jensen just said. The knowledge that he had naked photos leaked to the press was new to me and knowing that his privacy was invaded in such a cruel way makes me feel sick. No one–man or woman–should ever be objectified without their permission much like no one should be made to feel inferior because of their body type.

That knowledge, that he had something stripped from him much like I had my humility stripped from me over the years because of how my body looked, cements my decision. It makes me hurt for Jensen, much like I hurt for myself before I learned that my self-worth was so much more than what others thought of me. But even more than that, it makes me hurt for any other woman who ever felt they were less than. It makes me yearn for a future where no little girl will grow up being called chubby or plump in a derogatory way, where those same little girls saw women like me, who were healthy, curvy, and happy, and strive to be like me because they understand that beauty truly does come in all shapes and sizes and colors and genders.

Looking between the three sets of eyes that are peering back at me, I smile.

"I'm going to do it. I'm going to bare my ass to the world."

A chorus of "hell yesses" and "fuck yeahs" echo around the room from Ophelia and Jensen as Cole still looks on from the edge of the room.

"Babe, we are totally going to celebrate, but right now, please tell me I can go back upstairs and tell Rochelle that you're doing it! I'm going to make sure I'm damn well there for you every step of the way."

Ophelia's enthusiasm is contagious, and I love how happy she is for me. It makes me smile even wider as I nod, giving her silent permission to go share the news with her boss.

When I'm alone in the office with Jensen and Cole, and the energy level has dropped down by about five hundred degrees, I'm surprised when Cole speaks first. "Jay, mind if I steal your woman for a second?"

Jensen looks befuddled by the request, a look I'm sure I share, but he drops a quick kiss to my lips before excusing himself from the room, letting Cole know he'd meet him in the main locker room.

When it's just the two of us, I gesture to the chair in front of my desk as I retake mine behind my desk. "What's up, Cole? Something training-related I can help with?"

He lets out a long sigh, running a hand through his slightly shaggy hair. For as clean-cut as Jensen is with his short hair and closely trimmed beard, Cole is the opposite. Long, dark hair tumbles a few inches around his head, his wavy locks held off his forehead during games and training with pre-wrap, a non-adhesive yet tape-like fabric that is used commonly under athletic tape to prevent chafing and sticking.

"I just needed to apologize to you face-to-face. When the season first started, I may have made some insinuations about your body as a way to get under Jensen's skin. After Orlando, what happened there, and his reaction, I knew I needed to talk to you about it, too. It's been eating me up, and I've been feeling like a proper fool."

Looking at him over my desk, I'm surprised to see the sincerity in his eyes, and it speaks volumes. I had been afraid of Jensen when we first reunited at training and equally as apprehensive of Cole. But over the months as I've gotten to know both of them better, I've deduced that perhaps part of their attitudes, the misunderstanding and antics of their youth, is based on having to grow up faster than most others their age. While other kids were playing on their school teams and fighting over girls, these two were playing at near professional levels, traveling away from their families, and working toward representing their country.

"First day of training outside the bathroom after Jensen had confronted me?"

A self-deprecating grin eats up the lower half of his face. "Didn't realize those doors weren't soundproof."

I give him a little shrug. "Not quite."

"It was a dick move on my part, and I'm really sorry. I hope you'll be able to accept my apology one day."

"Already in the past, Cole."

He gives me another smile, this one reaching his eyes. "Appreciate it, Coach. And if I haven't said it in the past, I really am happy to have you as part of the team."

It's the first time he's called me Coach, usually choosing to just refer to me as Elle. It gives me a sense of pride, even a deeper feeling of comradeship to know that the final holdout of the players has embraced me as part of his team. I tell him as much as he stands to leave. He's almost out the door before he turns back into the room. "Also, for what it's worth, I'm really happy you gave Jensen another chance. He's a good lad, best damn friend I could have ever asked for."

He leaves, and I return to the once again quietness of my small space, wondering what the hell I've gotten myself into this time.

JENSEN WEST TO HOST TEAM PARTY AT STUNNING HOME ON BEACH

Gossip Nation Online: For Immediate Release

While the party is closed to the public, sources close to the action claim the party is in honor of girlfriend's upcoming photo shoot.

San Diego, CA, August 13– Inside sources have reported that Jensen West is having the party catered from local Mexican hotspot, Tacocat, a favorite of his conditioning-coach-turned-girlfriend, Eleanor Bigsby.

The source, wishing to remain anonymous, is quoted as saying, "I've never seen someone order so much food before in my entire life. Seriously, dude, he ordered tacos, rice, beans, chips, guac... like so much guac. And margaritas, too. Man, I wish I was invited."

END RELEASE

IN LESS THAN FORTY-EIGHT HOURS, my woman–and yes, she is *my* woman–is going to be posing for her first-ever magazine shoot. While her decision had been made the same day the email hit her inbox, we had spent hours over the last few weeks talking about the impact this would have on not only her future, but the future of countless young women who would see her photos, too.

She spent almost as much time with the marketing department as she did with the rest of the training staff; signing photography releases, setting expectations with the magazine on what she would and wouldn't do, and walking through the process of exactly what would happen when the photographer from *Sports Monthly* came to San Diego for the shoot. The added pressure of the shoot was stressing her the fuck out, and as we got closer and closer to the actual day where she would drop trou in front of a bunch of strangers, her anxiety continued to rev into overdrive.

But today, instead of focusing on that anxiety, we were letting loose and having fun as we celebrated her upcoming photoshoot.

Almost all the team is at my house–a first for me since buying the property. Players and their wives and girlfriends mill around the patio. To be clear, that is players with wives and players with girlfriends–none of my teammates have both. At least, none that I'm aware of. Kids swim in the pool, and laughter radiates throughout the space. Ophelia is here, as is Michelle, Eleanor's sister. Two more of Eleanor's friends are here, along with their significant others and children, too. Initially, I wasn't sure about having kids at my place, but when I mentioned to a few of the guys that I wanted to celebrate Eleanor with a team get-together this weekend to help put her at ease before her magazine shoot, they quickly decided my house was the place to do it. Hell, it's already like she's living here. But trust me, I don't mind. If I had it my way, she'd already be here permanently, but she insists on keeping her apartment, giving us space from one another when we need it.

But the thing is, I don't want space from Eleanor. I want her in my bed all the time. I want to see her each morning when I wake up, a tangled mess of hair and morning, sleep-filled eyes. I want to fall into bed with her each night, her arms and legs tangled around mine. I want to listen as she snores next to me so loudly that she wakes herself up, a habit she'll forever deny. I want every good morning and good night and every moment in between.

A group of women sitting off to the corner laugh, drawing my attention. Eleanor sits among them, commanding their attention as she does with everyone she meets.

One of the wives, a petite brunette, loops her arms around Eleanor's shoulders from behind. "I really wish I could get you into the WAG section in the stadium, but it has been awesome to watch you on the sidelines during the game!"

"What's the WAG section?" I hear her ask.

The brunette looks at me across the patio. "Jensen, you've been keeping her all to yourself, you greedy bastard!"

Laughter rings out around the area, coming from both the

players and their significant others. "The WAG section is where the wives, girlfriends, and kids sit during the games. We like to stick together. We can empathize with each other, knowing what our men are going through, joke about the cleat chasers that are constantly throwing themselves at their feet, and have a built-in support system that survives club transfers, retirement, and injury."

Another woman pipes up, one I haven't seen before. "You ladies totally should come join us one game as honorary members. Ophelia, don't you work for the team? And Elle, if you ever decide to hang up your coaching hat, know you'll be welcomed with open arms."

Seeing her fit in so seamlessly with the men who play such a huge part of my life and their families smacks me square in the chest. Sometimes, it's easy to forget how miserable I was before I met her. Even before I knew she was going to work alongside me, I knew there was something about her that would forever leave an indelible mark on my soul. Now, every day, she proves it more and more.

She's my forever.

And I'll do damn near anything to prove to her that I am hers.

Afternoon fades into evening, the laughter and fun never ending. The kids and some adults, have moved to a small fire pit, ingredients for s'mores being passed around.

While I love to cook, I wasn't quite up to the task of making food for a group this size, so I decided as soon as it was settled the party would be happening at my house to have the event catered. We filled ourselves earlier in the day with build-your-own tacos, chips, salsa, guac, and all the sides needed to create custom plates of nachos. Margaritas flowed as easily as the water trickling into the pool from the rock formation fountain on its edge.

Eleanor's childlike wonderment and love are always on display. She was the first to jump in the pool with the kids this afternoon, forever down to cuddle on the couch with a classic animated Disney movie, and generally would be the first person to jump in to making s'mores, not concerned if she ended up with sticky fingers full of melted chocolate and marshmallows.

I'm surprised that she isn't around the fire with the others, and after scanning my mind, I realize that I haven't seen her eat one thing all day. Sure, my attention hasn't fully been on her at all times throughout the day, but I'm sure had she eaten, she would have commented on the cilantro rice, extra jalapenos in the guac, and fresh corn tortillas brought in from the restaurant specifically with her in mind.

Finding her tucked in a corner, margarita glass between her fingers while she chats with her sister, I place a hand on her shoulder, garnering her attention. "Hey, Love. Can I talk with you inside for a sec?"

She excuses herself, following me into the house and into the small office off the side of the kitchen. I close the door behind her, and when she turns to face me, concern flares in her eyes. "Is everything okay?"

"Have you eaten today?"

"Huh?"

My voice comes out harsher than necessary, and she flinches as I speak. "Tell me, Eleanor. Have you. Eaten. Today?"

"Yeah, I had a bowl of Special K for breakfast."

"And lunch and dinner?"

I've caught her, and she knows it. Her shoulders sag, defeat and pain etched over her soft, round features.

"No." It's merely a whisper.

I don't respond, staring at her, daring her to tell me why. No matter what comes out of her beautiful mouth, I know I'm not going to like it.

"I don't want to look worse for the pictures than I already

know I'm going to. I didn't want to worry about extra pounds or bloat. It's just a few days."

My nostrils flare in anger–not at her, but at the world that made her feel as if she needed to starve herself before her photo shoot, at the fucking assholes who believe beauty is a one-size-fits-all mold, at the men who have surely talked down to her, making her believe that her curves were not perfection, that her soft stomach wasn't the most beautiful thing ever created.

I stomp across the office, grab her hand in mine, and drag her to the small couch that sits against one wall.

"Sit," I order. "Sit your ass on that couch and don't fucking move until I come back."

If she is startled by my outburst, she doesn't show it. Opting instead to comply with my demand, she sinks to the couch, keeping her back straight and her feet firmly planted on the plush carpet of the room.

I leave the room, keeping the door open behind me, and walk into the kitchen. Grabbing an oversized serving platter that sits empty on the island, I fill it with food until it is overflowing before stalking back to the office.

Eleanor's eyes widen as I return, slamming the door behind me with my free arm. I move to the couch, sitting next to her. "Get over here and sit on my lap."

"Wh...what?"

"You fucking heard me, Eleanor. Get over here and sit on my fucking lap."

She quickly scurries across the couch, dodging the plate of food that is precariously balanced in my hand. Askanced, she crawls onto my lap, sitting with her feet propped up on the couch next to us.

"Jensen, what are you doing?"

My arm loops behind her back, plate perched against the arm of the couch. With my free hand, I use my fingers to scoop up fragrant rice with a perfectly salted chip. I bring the chip to her pursed lips. "Open."

She doesn't immediately open, her eyes darting back and forth between the chip in my hand and my face. Almost a full minute passes until she finally breaks, parting her lips just enough for me to pass the chip into her mouth.

"If you think I'm going to stand by and let you starve yourself for even a fucking day, you've truly gone mad." I pull another chip from the plate, this one coated in salsa and cheese, and bring it to her mouth. This time, she doesn't hesitate, gently taking the chip from my fingers with her lips.

I feed her, bite after bite after bite as she sits on my lap, and the entire time I do, I tell her exactly what is on my mind. I tell her how gorgeous she is, how fucking exquisite her body is, how her attitude and mind are equally as compelling. How every minute of every fucking day, I want to slide between her legs and feast on her.

Another chip slides between her lips, leaving a hint of cheese sauce on her plump, bottom lip. I swipe across the lip I so badly want to bite and dip it into her mouth. Eleanor closes her full pout around my thumb, swirling her tongue around the digit before releasing it.

"You're so good to me, Jensen."

Satisfied she's gotten enough sustenance, I lessen my grip on the plate, bringing my hand instead to twirl through her hair. "You deserve it, my love."

It's a step closer to telling her my true feelings, to telling her that I am in love with her. For now, adding a strategically placed "my" to the endearment will have to do because while I do love her, I'm beyond terrified to tell her, afraid it will scare her away or that she won't return the sentiment. I continue to wind my hands in her hair, enjoying the quiet moment we've stolen away from the sounds of the party still going strong outside. "Love, you understand that you don't have to do this. No one would be upset if you decided you weren't comfortable with the entire thing."

Rearranging herself so she's straddling me, her arms loop around my neck as she stares earnestly into my eyes. "I want to do it. I know people will say things, and I'm prepared for that, but I want to do it. I *need* to do it–for everyone who has ever struggled with body image, yes–but also, I need to do it for myself. This has the ability to put any remaining doubt I have about myself behind me."

She drops her forehead to mine, placing an innocent kiss against my lips. Eleanor tries to pull away, but I hold her against me, refusing to let her go.

"Baby, if there is any doubt in your mind that you're not the most gorgeous woman in the world, if there is even an iota of doubt, then I'm not doing my job of worshiping every inch of your body every fucking day."

I claim her mouth with mine over and over and over again. My tongue sweeps against the seam of her lips, and she parts them, giving me access. Her nails trail gentle strokes over my scalp, sending pinpricks of desire through my body. I feel myself thicken in my board shorts, my cock already straining for escape. "You have no idea how bad I want to be inside of you right now."

Her hips rock against me, teasing my cock through the thin fabric of her suit bottoms. "Actually, I think I do."

A whoop of laughter erupts from outside as Eleanor continues to rub herself. Up and down, down and up. I can feel the heat of her cunt through our flimsy barriers–my beautiful, responsive woman, always so ready and eager for my cock.

Dropping one arm from my scalp, she brings her hand between us, holding herself on her haunches enough to snake her hand between her pussy and my dick. Working quickly, her hand fumbles with the string of my shorts before she works the velcro open, freeing my shaft from its constrictive hold.

Looking down between our bodies, she opens her mouth, allowing a trail of spit to fall from her lips, coating me with her saliva. Without removing her swimsuit cover-up, she reaches for her suit bottoms, pulling them to the side before positioning herself over my cock, sliding down onto me with one movement.

"Goddamn, woman. How are you always so wet and ready for me?"

She moans, lifting herself up and sliding back down as I bring my hands to her body, sliding beneath her cover-up to grip her hips. She's breathy and needy, exactly the way I love her most. "It's you, Jensen. You do this to me; you always do this to me."

My hands work in tandem with her body, hoisting her up and slamming her back down over and over and over. The precariously balanced plate on the edge of the couch crashes to the floor, leftover food scattering along with the shattered ceramic platter.

Neither of us bat an eye.

We're utterly lost in one another.

Lost in touching each other's bodies and feeling skin beneath our fingers, in the moans and pants that fill the quiet room around us. Lost in the electric pulse that swirls between us, and in the pull that binds us together.

"You were made for me, Eleanor. Your mind, your body, your tight light cunt...fuck, every single inch of you was made for me."

She's mine.

She's fucking mine.

"Harder," she pants against me. "I need you to fuck me harder, deeper. Please, I need more."

Removing my hands from her hips, I pull her chest flush with mine and piston into her. Over and over, and over I thrust forward, holding onto her body as I give her what she wants while chasing my own release.

A chorus of yeses and oohs fall from Eleanor's lips like a litany, a prayer lost for centuries only to be rediscovered when I'm buried deep within her walls.

"Yes, baby. Do you like that? Does your greedy little pussy like the way I feel inside of her? Do you like being my little toy?"

Nails claw at my body, and I'm certain she's leaving marks.

Good. I want her to mark me.

"Fuck, Jensen, don't you fucking stop. Don't you dare fucking stop!"

I'm close–so close–but I'll be damned if I finish before she does.

"Never, Princess. I'll never fucking stop until you explode around me first."

The door to the room swings open, Cole's head popping into the free space. "Oh, shit, my bad, mate."

I don't stop, knowing he can't see any of Eleanor's body, knowing that is reserved for my eyes only. Eleanor keeps going, also, too close to tipping over that edge to stop.

He goes to close the door, but I stop him, wanting him to watch, wanting him to see how magnificent Eleanor is as she comes apart, wanting her to see what her body does to another. He can have her sounds, but her body? That will only ever belong to me.

"What. Do you. Want?" My words are punctuated by thrusts.

"Jensen." My name is a plea as it comes out of Eleanor's mouth.

"You want him to watch you cum, baby? Want to look into his eyes as you soak me, knowing mine will be the only dick inside of you ever again?"

She moans, nails digging into me hard enough for little pricks of blood to pool at the surface of my skin. I lean into her ear, growling low so only she can hear me. "I'll kick him out if you want me to, but I think you like knowing he's watching. Don't you?"

"Yes..." Before she can continue, I slide out of her, turning her around and pulling her back down on my cock.

"Jay, man, I just wanted to tell you most people have gone, and I was about to head out." He thumbs over his shoulder toward the door.

I snarl, unaccepting of his dismissal. "Stay right fucking there and watch my little fuck toy, Cole. She wants you to watch, don't you, baby?"

Eleanor is bent nearly in half at the waist. I push her away before pulling her back to me, her perspiration-soaked hair moving with each and every thrust. "Yes...yes, I want him to watch."

"What else do you want?"

Cole's eyes are on Eleanor, watching as her body bucks back onto mine. His breathing hitches, and I don't have to look down to know he's hard.

Directly in front of me, Eleanor shakes her head. "No, I can't."

"Tell me," I command, my voice booming.

Her words rush out on an exhale, almost incoherent. From this view, I can't tell if Eleanor's eyes are on Cole's, but when she speaks, I immediately know they are. "I want him to touch himself, want to know I make other men feel as good as I make you feel."

Well, fucking hell. I didn't see that coming.

Cole's eyes snap to mine, uncertainty flaring behind them. I give him an imperceptive nod before tangling one hand in Eleanor's hair, snapping her head all the way back. "Then you better fucking watch."

She moans at the sensation, and when the sound leaves her

lips, Cole's hand reaches down to his dick, palming at it through his shorts. "Take them off," she pants. "I want to see you."

Christ, this woman. She's any man's wet dream.

This may be a fantasy for her, but somehow, I think it's something more. I think Eleanor needs this, needs to feel desired by more than just me, even if only for tonight. She needs to feel like her body is worthy before she puts it on display for the world to tear apart and criticize in some magazine spread. And if that is what she needs, who am I to deny her that?

I slow my thrusts, pulling her into my lap as my back rests against the couch. Still, with her back to my chest, she curls her legs beneath herself, balancing with her palms on my thighs. "Eleanor, do you want him to see more of you?"

She nods. "I need it. I need him to see me."

A silent understanding passes between Cole and me. He closes the door, crossing the small office to stand in front of her.

My best friend and I have shared women in the past, always a one-night-stand with an unknown woman neither of us ever had any intention of seeing again–never a woman one of us was serious about.

Never with a woman one of us loved.

I never had any intention of sharing Eleanor with anyone, not after that first night when I knew I was claiming her as mine, but if this is what she wants, what she needs, there is no one else I would implicitly trust to be our third.

Slowly, I continue to slide in and out of her pussy, her wetness sucking and slurping me back in. Cole tugs down on the waistband of his shorts, dropping them just low enough to free his dick. His hand wraps around his length, and I'm rewarded with Eleanor's pussy clenching my own cock.

My best friend comes even closer, prompting Eleanor to sit back on her knees as she gazes from his cock to his face. Momentarily, he releases himself, reaching out to Eleanor to pull her cover-up over her body, dropping it on the floor next to where he stands.

His hand returns to his cock, stroking himself, as mine travels up Eleanor's spine. I feel her tremble under my light touch, shaking when my fingers deftly untie the thin strip of fabric in the middle of her back, followed by the one secured around her neck.

She gasps as the flimsy fabric falls to the ground, breasts now on full display. Next, I work the tie on either side of her bottoms before letting the scrap of fabric fall around her.

"Is this what you want, little toy? To be on full display for Cole while I fuck you? For him to see your luscious breasts and bare pussy?"

She nods, a barely audible, breathy, "yes," the only thing she says.

Eleanor brings her hands to her chest, palming her own tits before rolling her nipples between her fingers. Cole's gaze stays transfixed on her breasts the entire time.

If this is what she needs, I'm damn well going to make sure she gets exactly that.

"Tell us how you want to finish, Love."

I slide out of her, slowly dragging the head of my cock over her clit before easily slipping back inside. "This is all for you. Whatever you want. Whatever you need, baby. You just have to tell me."

Licking his lips, Cole slowly peruses her body with a wolf's appetite, heat in his own gaze, his dick sliding through his hand the entire time.

She's staring directly ahead, but I know she's speaking to me when she talks. "I want you to make me cum. Both of you. I want to feel you fuck me while Cole rubs my clit."

I reach around her body, taking my turn to palm her tits. "Is that all?"

Her back arches, breasts pushing into my hands harder. I

pinch her nipples in response, hard enough for her to yelp. "Then…" she yelps again as I pinch her once more, "then I want to get on my knees like your little toy, and I want you both to cum on me."

Now I know for certain that I have died and gone to heaven.

"What do you say, brother?" I look at my friend, still standing just a foot away, still fisting his cock. "Should we give Eleanor what she wants?"

He grunts an unintelligible response as I begin to thrust into my woman with more force. Tentatively, he brings a hand to Eleanor's collarbone, trailing his fingers down her chest and over her tits. Cock still hard between his legs, he drops to his knees in front of me, continuing to trail his fingers down her soft stomach until he's resting his palm snugly against her pussy. I can tell the moment his fingers make contact with her clit because her back bows as moans and expletives fall from her dirty, filthy mouth.

"Damn, Jay, you know how to make her wet."

His opposite hand trails back up Eleanor's body, one large hand alternating between her tits. "This okay?"

I know he's asking Eleanor, making sure she is comfortable. Still, both her and I answer in unison with a reverent yes.

She careens towards the edge, four hands on her body instead of the normal two. Small beads of sweat trail her spine and slip between her breasts. I watch Cole as he catches one, and before he has the chance to wipe it away, Eleanor sucks his finger into her mouth.

I wish I could be that bead of sweat, licked from that finger and enveloped in her warm mouth.

"Fuck," Eleanor pants.

She's bucking her hips, riding my cock and the palm of Cole's hand. Keening into the abyss, she falls apart, head thrown back, pussy clenched around my cock. It's all I can do to keep myself from falling alongside her.

"Fuck, fuck, fuck!" she yells.

Still trembling, I urge her onto the floor, still of mind to have her watch for stray pieces of broken ceramic. While I'd love to give her more time, if I don't get her onto her knees now, her request is sure as hell not going to come true. And from the look on my friend's face, he is feeling the exact same way, holding on by a very thin thread.

"Do you still want us to mark you, toy? Want our cum on your pretty tits?"

Her eyes are blown wide, blissed out, as she looks up at me through long lashes and nods.

Cole and I both fist our dicks, pumping furiously towards release. We watch as Eleanor bites her lip, pulling it into her mouth. Her hands roam her body, over her tits, her stomach, dipping briefly between her legs. When she removes her hand, her fingers are glistening with moisture, and when she brings that hand back to her mouth, slipping her fingers inside and licking them clean, I lose it, spurts of cum falling over her tits and stomach as I unload onto her.

I drop to the ground behind her, pulling her arms behind her back and holding them in place while positioning her at my best friend. With my free arm, I snake around her body, grabbing a handful of the soft flesh of her inner thigh. Her body is glorious, all soft and round, but of every part of her, her thick, powerful thighs are my favorite.

She moans at the sensation, triggering Cole's release as more hot, sticky cum lands on her chest. Rope after rope fall across her, mixing with my own release, dripping down her stomach and falling on the floor between her knees.

Eleanor is beautifully wrecked, my perfect little toy, wanton and shameless and absolutely coated.

Turning her toward me, I find her discarded cover-up, wiping at the mess all over her skin. Cole catches my eye, tucking himself back into his pants, and makes a gesture toward the door. This time, when he walks out of the room, shutting the door behind him without a sound, I don't stop him.

Because now is my time.

My time to clean her.

To pull her into my arms.

And above all else, to make her feel as loved and as gorgeous as she truly is.

SOL STADIUM CLOSED TO THE PUBLIC FOR PRIVATE EVENT

San Diego Sol Football Club: For Immediate Release

While the stadium is open daily for guest tours, a private event has temporarily suspended operations.

San Diego, CA, August 15- A closed photo shoot happening within its walls has prompted extra security measures at the stadium. Meanwhile, the team has been relocated to a local auxiliary facility, granting Sports Monthly an added layer of privacy for their Bare It All shoot with Coach Eleanor Bigsby.

Team owner and father of Eleanor, Maxwell Bigsby is quoted as saying, "This is an unprecedented time not only for my daughter but for the club as well. Sports Monthly has gone above and beyond to make sure all parties involved with the shoot have shown the utmost respect for Eleanor, our staff, and our club."

END RELEASE

ELEANOR

16.

THROUGHOUT MY LIFE, I've certainly done some pretty stupid things. Actually, I've done a lot of them.

Like the time I was eight and was certain I could fly if I just jumped from high enough on our rickety, old, wooden swing set that was in our backyard. I pumped my little legs as hard as possible, swinging higher and higher and higher, pink cape tied to my neck like I was some kind of child superhero, before letting go of the chains holding the swing.

Or the time I was fifteen and tried to climb from my second-story bedroom window to meet up with friends to smoke pot when I was grounded. I successfully made it onto my roof, halfway down the trellis with California Honeysuckle vines winding their way before it snapped, sending me and my mom's favorite flowers tumbling to the ground.

Both times, I ended up with broken bones and one hell of a story to recount to anyone who would listen.

I've always chased that adrenaline. Skydiving, whitewater rafting, even swimming with sharks on a family vacation, I've done it all. Never have I met a rollercoaster that I didn't like, and I'm always looking for something to give me that high, loving the feeling of doing something that scares most other people.

But as I sit in nothing but a black silk robe, hair and makeup impeccably done, with dozens of people standing around me, I know I've truly lost my damn mind.

Not knowing the entertainment industry, I never knew how many people were present at a magazine photo shoot. Of course, the photographer is there as well as a makeup artist and hair stylist, but there is also a producer, prop stylist, set designer, and production coordinator.

Hell, I'm going to be naked for these pictures aside from a few strategically placed soccer balls and pieces of equipment, and the photos are being taken right here at the stadium. Why the hell do we even need a prop stylist and set designer?

Clutching a cup of coffee so tightly that my knuckles are white, I listen as Ophelia and Rochelle discuss the plans with the members of the magazine.

I begged Jensen to let me skip breakfast this morning, not out of wanting to cut calories or appear thinner than normal, but because I was terrified that if I ate even a morsel of something, that it would come right back out in front of this room full of people.

He wasn't hearing any of it, insisting I eat and going as far as to sit next to me, feeding me forkful after forkful from my plate until he was satisfied, much like he did over the weekend at the get-together he threw for me at his house.

Thinking back to that night makes my spine tingle, and momentarily, I forget that I'm just a few minutes away from baring myself in front of a room full of strangers.

Jensen did something magical for me that night. I'm not sure he knows it, but having him praising me and filling my mind with words of affirmation as he fucked me gave me the confidence I needed to go forward with this photo shoot. I had been ready to back out more times than I could count up until that moment, until he allowed me to take my pleasure from his body. But when he gave me full control, all the while telling me how beautiful I was, it was like something inside me snapped. I actually felt beautiful, truly desired and wanted, for maybe the first time in my entire life.

It was the ultimate high, an adrenaline rush I hadn't known I had been chasing for twenty-two years.

I was so lost in the moment that I hadn't even heard Cole open the door. He could have stayed there the entire time, silently watching as I found my release on top of Jensen, and I probably never would have noticed.

And Jensen could have let him.

But he didn't.

He invited Cole in, with my permission, knowing what I needed in that moment more than I knew for myself.

The desire, the passion, the lust.

It was everything I needed to feel confident enough to do this photo shoot, and while it was sex between three people, it was almost as if it wasn't sex at all. It was a silent understanding between the three of us, the two of them giving me what I wanted–what I *needed.*

Having two men as beautiful as Jensen and Cole at my disposal was extremely gratifying–powerful even. They made me feel sexy as their hands roamed my body, authoritative as they took my direction, fulfilling what I needed.

And while I don't think it's an experience I ever would have pursued or an experience I will want to have again, I'll forever be indebted to both of them for the moment they shared not only with me but with one another, too.

I had heard the stories of the Jensen and Cole of the past, heard the tales of their wild nights, sharing women, and even light drug use they fell into during their younger years. Jensen himself had told me about the bad reputation he had, about the equally poor attitude that came with it, and how he was actively trying to turn that around, wanting to make more of himself as part of a lasting legacy of his years as a footballer.

Footballer…hell, even his vocabulary and hold of the game have begun to wear off on me.

"Five-minute warning!" a voice calls from across the room.

Ophelia excuses herself from the conversation happening, coming over to stand next to where I am seated in one of those cliche little folding chairs you always see on movie sets. Hell, if I ever decide to do one of these again, maybe I'll have them write it in my contract that I will only agree if I get my name bedazzled across the back in true diva fashion. "How ya holding up, babe?"

My stomach does a little lurch, and I take a deep breath to keep my breakfast from ending up on the floor. "I'd rather be in stirrups at the gynecologist."

"Oof, that good?" She plucks the coffee cup from my hands, setting it down on the small table that doubled as a staging area for hair and makeup. I protest, but before any words can leave my mouth, she is snapping at someone, demanding they bring me a large, peppermint tea. "Always better for stomach issues. The caffeine in that coffee will just give you the shits on top of the jitters."

I manage a weak laugh, graciously taking the cup that is thrust in front of me. Long swallows of the hot liquid coat my throat, and miraculously, it does seem to settle my stomach, even if just a bit.

My makeup artist–a fantastic soul by the name of DeAndre who uses They/Them pronouns, owns two French bulldogs that travel with them all over the country, and drives a vintage Chevrolet Impala–returns to the table, gently scolding me for drinking from the cup before reapplying my lipstick.

Seriously, there is so much makeup caked on my face that if the Titanic were to hit me, I'd take it down faster than the stupid iceberg that actually did the job.

My eyes are dark and smoky with a hint of glitter. Bronzer and highlighter sculpt my cheekbones, and my lips are a red that is so deep, it's almost black. If I were anywhere outside of a photoshoot, I'd look like a clown. Yet somehow here, it makes me look good.

Much to my dismay, the shoot is a closed set, and despite my near begging, Jensen is not allowed to be here with me. It's not that I can't do this without him, but I simply don't want to.

The man does things to me, makes me feel more beautiful than I've ever felt, makes me feel desired. *Loved.*

Across the room, the producer of the shoot calls everyone to attention, and a flurry of activity begins. Lights flip on, the photographer readies her camera, and I begin to sweat profusely.

Seriously, every pore of my body goes into overdrive. I feel it on my brow, across the top of my lip…hell, I even feel a bead of sweat drip down my ass crack.

"Holy shit, what the fuck did I get myself into?"

Ophelia wraps her arm around me. "You're going to do great, babe. Normally, I'd tell you to just picture everyone in their underwear, but I don't know if it would have the same senti-ment in this situation, seeing as how you're going to be in less than yours."

DeAndre brings a thin sheet of tissue paper-like material to my face, blotting and dabbing the sweat that has sprung across my skin. "Baby, you're a stunner, but if you don't stop fucking up your makeup, we're going to throw hands!"

I laugh, apologizing for messing up their hard work. "I just really wish Jensen could be here with me."

Squealing, Ophelia reaches into the pocket of her black skinny jeans. "Fuck, I almost forgot. He asked me to get this to you when I ran into him on my way here." She slips a small slip of paper to me, giving me a small, reassuring smile. "You really are going to knock 'em all dead."

The producer, an older lady named Sandy with long gray hair, thick red-rimmed glasses, and head-to-toe black clothing approaches. "I know you've gone over the details many times, but if during this process today there is anything I can do to make you more comfortable, please just let me know, and I will do my best to accommodate it. While I've never been in your shoes specifically in this capacity, I do know how unnerving it can be. Every person here is designed to make you look and feel your best. Take a few deep breaths, and when you're ready, come on over, robe still on."

Sandy walks away, and I take her advice, breathing in through my nose before letting long exhales out through my mouth. Still clutching the paper in my hand, I finally allow myself to unclench my fingers around the small piece of Jensen I have here with me today.

My Eleanor,

You're amazing every day, but today, in particular, I'm extra proud of you for putting fear aside to do this.

See you tonight, sweetheart.

Your Jensen

THE FIRST GENUINE SMILE I'VE HAD ALL DAY PLAYS across my lips as I trace his words with my fingertips. I feel ready—confident. He's instilled that in me, that feeling of being able to conquer the world, flaws and all. I read the note one more time, the grin on my face growing wider. I want to drop my robe and sashay across the floor naked as the day I was born.

I'm not going to do that, but I think about it.

I call out to Sandy, a plan forming in my mind with exactly how I can repay him for all the strength and bravery he has given me, for the love he has shown me and the intimacy he's brought to my life.

He's going to love it. And he's going to lose his mind.

SAN DIEGO SOL TO CELEBRATE MULTIPLE TEAM VICTORIES.

San Diego Sol Football Club: For Immediate Release

Team to welcome local community to join in celebration this weekend.

San Diego, CA, October 21- As the playoffs quickly approach, San Diego Sol look to continue their run to the trophy while coach and local celebrity, Eleanor Bigsby, looks to improve the treatment of women throughout the professional sports industry. The community is invited to attend Sol in the Park this weekend to rally around the team. Opportunities for autographs and pictures will be available, as well as entertainment and education.

Maxwell Bigsby is quoted as saying, "As I continue my tenure with San Diego Sol, I look forward to partnering with local organizations that push for fair and equal treatment of women in athletics, while fostering strong bonds with children within our community."

END RELEASE

After our absolutely abysmal performance last season, it is no surprise that the community is rallying behind our recent streak of good luck. Throughout San Diego, billboards of our team line the freeways, people place yard signs on their lawn cheering us on, and at the request of our marketing team, we've been ramping up meet-and-greets.

But today, at our team's big pre-playoff party, we're celebrating more than just our team because yesterday, Eleanor's photos debuted not only in print, but online, too.

I wasn't surprised when she made everyone fall in love with her during her photo shoot, getting comfortable to the point that they asked her to do an interview for the magazine, too. I only wish I could have been there in person to support her as she battled with anxiety in the minutes leading up to that first snap of the camera. Yeah, I would have killed to see her beautiful body in all its glory while she was primping and posing, but even more than that, I just wanted to be there to see her succeed.

Besides, she gives me more than enough of that gorgeous ass, those sinful thighs, and that lucious tummy every day. Still, I'm always craving more.

It's also no surprise that her pictures turned out absolutely magnificent. While only a select few made the magazine, I was fortunate enough to see each and every one. I may even have a flash drive in my possession of the entire shoot, and I am not ashamed to admit that fact.

Her hair and face in the photos remind me of the night we first met–all wild and crazy, smoky and sultry. They range from fun and flirty to downright seductive, and while those are some of my favorites, I chose to pick a less suggestive pose to hang proudly from the back of my locker.

Every day I hang it, and every day, Eleanor comes behind me, taking it down and confiscating it like it's contraband in a maximum security prison. She says she's not ashamed of the pictures, that they made her feel powerful, but that it's inappropriate to have it on display in the locker room. This is just one time where she and I will have to agree to disagree.

Also, she has no idea how many copies of that single photo I had printed, knowing she would protest.

In it, she stands with her back to the camera, two strategically placed soccer balls covering the round globes of her ass. Hair tumbles down her back as she arches to look at the camera over her shoulder. At her insistence, nothing but minor touch ups were done on the photos, correcting fly away hairs or smudged makeup, and I love that when I look at them, I can see every curve, every slight dimple on her thigh, every inch of her skin that is slightly a different color where stretch marks mar her porcelain skin.

God, she is my everything.

And while I hope she already knows that, I'm going to tell her tonight.

We arrive together at the park where the event is being hosted, as we so often do nowadays, and although the afternoon is casual, I insisted on hiring a driver for the occasion. This day belongs to her just as much as it belongs to me and the players on the team.

Already, kids are playing on mini soccer pitches, taking turns trying to score on one another. A few even run around in mini replicas of my kit, and for the first time in my life, I imagine what it would be like to have one of those of my own–a mini combination of Eleanor and myself with her wild, crazy red curls and my light blue eyes.

It's a slightly unsettling feeling, but not completely unwanted, and that should scare the shit out of me more than anything.

But it doesn't.

Not even a full minute passes before Eleanor and I are pulled in different directions, nothing but a quick peck on the lips before we part ways. She's engulfed in a crowd of wives and girl-friends as they all praise her on her pictures, telling her how awesome she looked, how they wish they could have her confidence.

I tell her daily how beautiful she is, how amazing both her mind and body are, but still, I know the acceptance from other women means the world to her.

As I get passed around from fan to fan, taking pictures and signing autographs, she's never out of my sight. I even see her signing a few of her own pictures at times, posing for selfies alongside men and women alike. I won't say I like seeing men put their arms around her, pulling her in closer than necessary for pictures, but I know she can handle herself, and I refuse to let my jealousy ruin her day or mine.

Eleanor spends time with young women who are interested in pursuing careers in athletics. She speaks with members of several organizations that are vendors at the event, talking about spreading her own message of body positivity far and wide.

All around us, families play games, get pictures with the team's mascot, and fill up on swag decked out in team colors.

Finally, I get a minute alone with her, pulling her inside a small concession stand usually reserved for little league games, before pulling her into my arms. "I've missed you," I whisper into her ear.

Grinning up at me through those tantalizingly long lashes of hers, she responds, "Missed me? I've been here with you the entire time."

I lean down, kissing her lips and not wanting to stop. "You can be in the same damn room as me, Eleanor, but if you're not *with me*, not in my arms, I miss you."

"Well, in that case, I guess it's a good thing I'm in your arms right now."

Wishing I could keep her right here forever, but knowing we can't escape for long, we return to the crowds of people hand-in-hand. A local band plays music, I catch several of the guys in line at the multiple food trucks parked on the property, and I even spy Coach James with his two young daughters.

I used to hate these damn events. Showboating in front of the community like a damn pony, faking smiles and conversations all to make sure we stay on the good side of our fans. But today, not only is it tolerable, it's dare I say...enjoyable. And it's all thanks to the woman at my side.

Our fingers are linked together as we continue to mingle with the crowd, making our way towards where the youngest kids are playing. We stand, watching them run back and forth, kicking–and mostly missing–the ball all the while giggling and squealing with delight. I wrap my arms around her from behind, inhaling the fresh, cotton scent lingering on her skin. "You ever want one of those?"

"Eh. If it happens for me down the line, it happens. If not, I don't think I would be devastated. Honestly, I've never felt that strong maternal pull like some women do."

"So, what you're saying is we'll be cool Uncle Jensen and Auntie Eleanor. We can have all the fun with our friends' kids during the day, and then we can pass them back off to their parents at the end of the night, retire to our nice, quiet home, and fuck like bunnies all damn night."

She laughs, shushing me at the same time. Eleanor points to the small kids, not paying us any mind. "Impressionable minds are close by. But yeah, I like that idea. I *really* like that idea."

From out of nowhere, Ophelia runs onto the mini-pitch, squealing as she runs around, lightly kicking the ball away from the children as they all chase her. Eleanor laughs at her friend. "And there's the biggest kid of them all."

"Think we can take her?"

"With you on my team?" A giant smile breaks out across her pretty face. "Let's do this!"

We enter the small, fenced in area, and I quickly come up behind Ophelia, easily knocking the ball away from between her feet. I run down the tiny field, dribbling the ball between my feet while paying no attention to Ophelia's cries of me playing unfairly.

"Eleanor, think fast!"

I pass the ball to her, and after only a quick stutter, she gains control of it, holding it under her right foot. Tiny kids swarm towards her, laughing and giggles filling the air. They're almost at her, clamoring towards her feet. I holler at her. "Shoot the ball!"

Rolling her foot off the ball, she takes one last look at the kids before looking at the small child in the net. Pulling her foot back in almost slow motion, she brings it back to connect with the ball, sending it to the right as the kid in goal jumps to the left like a cat pouncing on a ball of yarn.

It rolls into the back of the net as I jog toward her, picking her up and twirling her in my arms as half the kids cheer, the other half sulking off, feeling wounded by losing out on defending the goal.

"My first official goal! Better watch out or I'll be coming for your job." She pokes me in the ribs, making me squirm from the ticklish sensation that courses through my body.

I retaliate, grabbing her sides and playfully tickling up and down until she begs me to stop. "You only made that goal because you had a great assist, Princess. Don't go inflating your ego too much just yet."

Ophelia jogs up next to us. "That was absolutely *not* fair."

Eleanor laughs at her friend while I simply shrug my shoulders in a *sometimes life isn't fair* gesture.

The girls scurry off together, something about Eleanor needing to grab something from Ophelia's car, and I use the opportunity to search the crowd for my best friend who has been noticeably absent today.

Not being able to find him, I make my way toward the refreshments that have been set up for the day. When I'm almost to the table, a voice I am all too familiar with calls out to me.

"Oh, honey, there you are! Jensen, it's simply been too long!"

Cecelia Van Hutchinson.

Fuck my life.

I turn to face the biggest mistake of my life, not managing to crack a smile when we're face to face.

It doesn't faze her that I am unhappy to see her as her arms come up to wrap around my neck in a sickeningly tight hold.

"What the hell are you doing here?"

"Like I need an excuse to visit my *favorite* man on such a special day?" She stretches out the word favorite, playing with it as it rolls off her tongue. Cecelia thinks it's cute. It's actually annoying as hell.

I step back, managing to peel her arms off of my neck. "I am not your man, Cecelia."

She laughs, a haughty, slightly jilted sound that grates on my nerves. "Oh, Jensen, baby," she tries to purr, but it comes out sounding more like a dying pigeon choking on a crumb of stale bread. "I know you've been working through your silly, little mid-life crisis with the boss's daughter, and I've been off *performing*, but it's time for you to stop playing house with that child. It's time for you to come home to a real woman, don't you think?"

My tone is laced in venom when I bring myself to speak again. I close the space between us, making sure only she can hear my words. "Listen, Cecelia, you might think what I'm going through is some mid-life crisis bullshit, but what I'm actually doing is falling in love with someone who gives a rat's ass about me, someone who believes in me, and someone whom I believe in fiercely. Had you truly had an ounce of love in your body, perhaps you would have thought twice before leaking private pictures of me to a magazine, or at least had an ounce of remorse in your body for your actions."

I expect her to retort, to be angry, or to stomp away in a mock fit of rage. What I don't expect is for her to lean into me, put her palms on my chest, and fuse her lips to mine.

The feeling is so unexpected that I momentarily freeze, not moving until I feel her tongue sweeping inside my own mouth.

I push her away, using slightly more force on a woman than I should, but the damage is already done, and both Cecelia and I know it as we hear a broken voice utter my name from behind me.

Cecelia smirks in the direction of the voice before turning back to me, batting her creepily long eyelashes at me. Seriously, it's like the woman has daddy long legs glued to her face, coated under about twenty coats of mascara. Looking at her now, I'm not sure what I ever saw in the woman. I can't even say that she is just a pretty face because honestly, she's got nothing on Eleanor.

"I'll see you at home, lover boy," she says, wiggling her fingers in a wave in Eleanor's direction before slinking off into the crowd.

I turn to face Eleanor, her bright green eyes glassy as tears spill over onto her round, full cheeks. "Baby, listen to me..."

My sentence is cut off before I can continue.

"No, Jensen, you listen to me." She keeps her voice low so as to not bring attention to our private conversation, but still, several sets of eyes land on us.

"Clearly, whatever this thing was between us..." she motions her hand back and forth between our chests before letting out a long sigh, shaking her head back and forth, "you asked me to give you a chance and the only thing I asked for in return was that you didn't break my heart. I should have known better than to believe that you wouldn't because today, you most certainly did."

She thrusts a small, wrapped gift into my hands as tears continue to fall from her eyes. "I hope you find happiness, Jay."

I grab her wrist, pulling her back into me. "It wasn't what it looked like, Love."

Breaking free of my hold and now not caring who hears, her voice raises. "From where I stood, it looked like you were whispering to her right before you had your tongue down her throat, and I'm pretty certain you can't deny that. See you later, *lover boy*." She throws the taunt from Cecelia back into my face like a cream-filled pie at a carnival clown.

Ophelia's quickly at her side, gently cradling Eleanor in her arms and ushering her away from me while telling her it will be okay. They're several steps away when I call out, "Eleanor, wait!"

Her footsteps stop, and my heart soars with hope that she'll turn back around, that she'll talk to me and allow me to tell her what truly happened, that everything will be okay and we can go back to how we were.

But hope is foolish, and I know that more than the rest.

Because she doesn't come back–doesn't even turn around.

She simply walks away.

REUNITED AND IT FEELS SO GOOD.

Gossip Nation: For Immediate Release

After nearly a year apart, Jensen West and Cecelia Van Hutchinson are spotted together.

San Diego, CA, November 6- Following a separation of almost one year, soccer star West and pop star Van Hutchinson were recently seen together at the San Diego Sol's community-wide party celebrating the team's upcoming playoff run.

Cecelia Van Hutchinson is quoted as saying, "The distance was hard, so very hard, but I am beyond thrilled to be together with Jensen once again. We truly are two halves of the same puzzle, and we are much better together."

END RELEASE

I'VE NEVER MINDED my small apartment, but after months of basically living with Jensen, the walls of my small, one-bedroom space have become almost claustrophobic. While the walls of his large home were sparse, mine are covered with artwork, pictures of friends and family, and strings of fairy lights. Still, when I look around my apartment, it still seems bare.

Scattered takeout boxes are strewn across my coffee table, bunched-up tissues litter the area surrounding my couch, and I have permanent bags under my eyes from lack of sleep and excessive crying.

I wanted to run after it first happened, after I saw Jensen with that absolutely stunning woman at the park that day, after I saw his lips on hers. And I suppose I did run to an extent, not waiting to hear what sorry excuse he would try to spin to get himself out of it. I shoved the photo album I had made for him into his arms, turned around, and left.

I wanted to never show my face at the stadium again. I wanted to bury my head in the sand or at least escape to a tropical island where men weren't allowed and each woman owned a private beachfront bungalow and four cats.

But I didn't.

I held my head high, went to work every day, although I

spent more time than not crying in the bathroom, and did my best to avoid Jensen West at any cost necessary.

It has been oddly reminiscent of our early days around each other. An odd tap dance of avoidance where we both had so much to say, yet neither of us were brave enough to make first contact.

As if the breakup wasn't bad enough on its own, what came next has been just as gut wrenching–waking up each morning and grabbing for my phone to text him before remembering that he isn't mine anymore, trying a new dessert and wanting to share a bite with him only to recall that we don't share meals anymore.

Today marks two weeks, but it still feels just as raw.

I miss him *so* damn much.

I had dated before Jensen, even had a few relationships, but I was never lucky enough to find that one person to fall in love with. He was my first.

And I hoped he would be my last.

Looking around my living room, I toss another used tissue on the floor. We're still in the playoffs, inching our way toward the final, and tomorrow, we leave for a two-game stretch on the road.

"Fuck, I really need to clean this place up," I mutter to no one.

As if the universe knows I've now stooped to the level of talking aloud to myself, my doorbell rings.

"Open up!" Ophelia calls from the other door.

"Let us in!" Michelle says at the same time.

This is what I get for living in a moderately-priced building without an intercom system and a fancy doorman.

Groaning, I peel myself from the coach, a weekend's worth of stale clothing sticking to my body and matted hair sticking out in all directions.

They knock again, growing impatient.

"I'm coming, I'm coming. Can't a woman wallow in her own filth and self-pity alone?"

Both women barge into my apartment the second the door is open nearly knocking me out of the way.

Ophelia takes one sweeping look around. "You want to get her in the shower or clean this mess?"

"I used to bathe with her as a child; I can get her in there if you're good out here. Seriously, Elle, I've been in a kitchen that has been health code violated that didn't look this bad."

My sister nudges me towards my bathroom, closing the door behind us once we're both inside. She points at my chest, "You," then to the shower, "in there now."

I let out a huff, but she gives me a glare that makes me feel more like she's my mother than my sister.

"You guys didn't have to come."

"Yeah, we did. Now get in the shower before I physically strip you down and wash you. I know you're sad, but you will not wallow in filth every weekend for the rest of your life."

I start removing clothes while the water warms, all while my sister sits perched on the closed toilet seat. When I'm finally behind the curtain of my shower, I feel like I am capable of speaking. "You know, I'm not just sad. I loved him, Chelle. Fuck, I still love him."

She lets out a sigh, and while she doesn't speak words, her meaning is clearly defined in that single sigh.

It says, *I know.*

I've been there.

And *I'm sorry.*

I continue, feeling brave with my opaque shower curtain shielding me. "I just...I thought it was going to be forever with him, you know? We laughed together, we shared our painful histories with each other. Hell, he made me love my job, made my dreams shift from wanting to work for the NFL to staying with Sol." Tears stream down my face, only disguised by the water. "He still calls me every day. I haven't answered once. Aside from our limited interactions at work, I haven't spoken one word to him, and I swear, Michelle, every day it kills me just a little bit more. I mean, she's the one who sold naked photos of him to the press. How can someone just forgive that?"

I hear the bathroom door open before my sister hollers out into the apartment. "Ophelia, get in here!"

Footsteps approach, and soon there is a third body in my tiny apartment bathroom. "Elle, tell her what you just told me."

After repeating the story again, the bathroom falls silent, and I have to stick my head out from behind the curtain to make sure both women are still in the room with me. My sister sits, still perched on the toilet lid while Ophelia sits on my single sink vanity, ass fully seated in the basin of the sink.

"You really haven't talked to him at all?" Ophelia asks.

I shake my head as she hands me a towel before I return to the confines of my shower stall to dry off.

"I know you don't want to hear this, but I really think you should hear him out," my sister says. I scoff, but she continues before I can interject. "I've only seen you together in person twice, but Elle, the man adores you. He looks at you like you're the only woman in the room when you're together."

Ophelia cuts in, "It's true, babe. He looks at you like you're a glass of iced tea on a hot summer's day, and he's simply gotta drink you down. Like you're the perfect wave to surf, notes on a scale strung together to make the perfect chord…"

"Enough with the metaphors." I pull back the shower curtain, fluffy towel wrapped around my now clean body. "He was very clear with his decision. It's kinda hard not to be when your lips are vacuum-sealed to someone else's mouth."

My sister speaks next. "But, Eleanor, if he wanted to walk out of your life, he would have gone. You've been holding the door open for him, making it easier to walk away, and he still hasn't. He's still trying to talk to you, to get to you. He's putting in effort, Elle. What if this really is some kind of twisted misunderstanding? Isn't effort worth more than perfection?"

I roll the words around in my brain as I change into fresh clothing, and I'm still considering them as I fall back onto the couch surrounded by my sister and best friend. Thanks to Ophelia's hard work, the floor is no longer full of used tissue landmines. The coffee table is clear of clutter, a clean, cotton-scented candle burns on the kitchen island, and there are cut-and-bake cookies cooling on the stovetop.

The three of us sit in silence, squished on my little couch as some cheesy comedy streams on the small television. I can't be bothered to pay attention, couldn't tell you any of what is happening on screen, but from the giggles emanating from the other two, I can tell that it must be good.

Michelle pushes up from the sagging cushions, grabbing more than enough cookies to feed three women, and sets them down on the low coffee table in front of us. She and Ophelia each pop one into their mouths, and when I don't move to join them, Ophelia picks up another, almost forcefully holding it to my lips. "You've gotta eat, babe."

My sister nods in agreement. "Normally, I wouldn't agree that cookies are part of a balanced meal, but...what the hell." She grabs another from the tray, inhaling it in one bite. "So, what do you say, Elle? Are you going to at least hear him out?"

I sigh for what feels like the seven hundredth time today, running a hand through my freshly-washed hair. "I honestly don't know. I want to believe that you're both right, that it is some kind of misunderstanding, but how could it have been? If I talked with him, and it turned out he really was just using me for sex, that all of this was some sort of fucked up game...I don't know that my already broken heart could handle it."

Pulling me into her arms, I relish in the human contact I've been starved of since leaving Jensen two weeks ago. Ophelia scooches herself closer, turning me into a full on Eleanor sandwich between two of the most important women in my life.

"Promise you'll at least think about it?" my sister asks.

I nod against her body. "I'll think about it."

Ophelia squeals, looping her arms around both of us. "Thank God, Elle! I need you to get back together. I never even got to use your celebrity nickname I invented!"

"Nickname? What nickname?"

"Yeah, you know all the best celebrity couples have nicknames. Bennifer, Brangelina, Kimye, TomKat…"

As I so often do with my best friend, I cut her off before she can continue. "One, I want to know what crazy nickname you concocted, and two, notice that none of those couples are together anymore?"

"One," she responds sassily, "it's Jelenor. And secondly, don't you forget that Bennifer may have split, but not only are they together again, they're *married*! Totally bringing back the early 2000s!"

A giggle erupts from somewhere deep within my chest, from the empty cavity I didn't think would ever be filled with laughter again. The two are utterly ridiculous, and for that, I absolutely love them.

"So, what you're saying is that I might still have a chance at true love?"

"Fuck yes! Bring on Jelenor!"

I struggle to remove myself from their embraces, snagging another cookie for myself, with the first true smile on my face in two weeks.

Tomorrow after practice, I'm going to talk to Jensen.

SAN DIEGO SOL ADVANCE TO SEMIFINALS.

Gossip Nation: For Immediate Release

Young talent and tenured players have worked together to propel Sol towards the final.

San Diego, CA, November 6- After falling short last season, the San Diego Sol is only one match away from their third Major League Soccer final. While pundits believe the combination of fresh faces and veteran players has been the base of success for the team, Coach Calder believes it is at the core, the heart and Sol of the team, that has made all the difference.

Coach James Calder is quoted as saying, "Throughout the season, this team has shown an extreme amount of heart, bringing their best to each training session and game. They have worked tirelessly to come together as a solid force, and I look forward to watching them progress toward the final."

END RELEASE

Over the last two weeks, I've been a powder keg of anger seconds away from exploding. I've been fighting with my teammates, barely talking with my family and friends, and have spent more time than not trying to solve my problems with bottle after bottle of Macallan.

Worst of all, Eleanor will not so much as glance in my direction.

And for once in my life, I truly haven't done anything wrong.

Sitting on my patio, I stare at the ocean in the distance. A light breeze creates a chill in the air, and I can't help but think how much better the night would be if Eleanor were here, my arms draped around her shoulders as she curled into me. Having her in my arms feels like home, and that's a feeling I didn't know I was longing for until I met her.

I used to subscribe to the idea that commitment wasn't for me. The whole idea of one woman for the rest of my life was terrifying. But over the last few months I've learned that the very opposite is true. Besides, there is no such thing as the next best thing when you've already discovered the perfect woman.

Unable to make my body move from the plush lounge chair until long after the sun has fully set, I finally force myself inside when the breeze becomes cooler, heading right back to the half-empty bottle of scotch on my kitchen island. Bottle poised over my empty glass, my eyes catch on something off to the side of the island.

A small, brown, wrapped package.

The gift from Eleanor.

I had been so consumed with stewing in my own sadness that I completely forgot about it. Filling my glass almost to the brim, I place the bottle back on the counter, then pick up my glass in one hand and the package in the other.

My feet move of their own accord, a separate entity than the rest of my body. Before my brain can catch up, I find myself in the office, sitting on the same couch where I shared Eleanor with Cole.

It was the most intimate moment of my life, feeling her clench around my cock while he toyed with her clit. I could feel her letting go of any remaining walls around herself at that moment, fully giving herself to me, even while another man was in the room with us.

Inhaling deeply, I search for any remaining trace of her scent in the room but am left disappointed when only stale air assaults my nose.

I gulp down half my glass, setting it on the floor next to me before carefully opening the brown butcher paper wrapping, treating it as an extension of whatever may be hidden inside. When the mystery item is finally unwrapped, a small, black book stares back at me.

I flip it over in my hands, both the front and back free of any telling markings. Holding my breath, not sure what to expect, I flip open the cover to a plain white page with Eleanor's handwriting in gold scrawled across the page.

My Jensen,

I never knew what I was missing until you came into my life. Since trusting you with my heart, almost everything about me has changed. Yet today, I'm more myself than I ever have been before.

Thank you for giving me the confidence I never knew I was lacking, the laughter I never knew I was missing, and the desire to explore this crazy world with you by my side.

Thank you for loving me.

Love,

Your Eleanor

I CAN'T BRING MYSELF TO TURN THE PAGE TO SEE what the rest of the book contains. Closing the cover and setting the book next to me on the couch, I reach down to my glass, bringing it to my lips and quickly polishing off the amber liquid inside.

She *loves* me.

Well…loved me.

And Cecelia fucking Van Hutchinson had to go and fuck it all up.

Picking up the book again, I quickly reread her words before turning the page.

I'm absolutely speechless at what I find.

Picture after picture of Eleanor fills the small album. I recognize them as pictures from the day of her photo shoot, but there is something different about these. While the majority of pictures from the shoot were taken on the field, it's immediately apparent that these are special. These were taken just for me.

In the first, she's sitting in the locker room, back to the camera and a sultry stare on her face. Straddling a chair, her hair is pulled on top of her head. Eleanor isn't naked in this picture, it's nowhere near as sexy as some of the others I've seen of her. But this…well fuck me, it might just be the best photograph ever taken because in it, Eleanor is wearing nothing but my jersey and a tiny pair of lace panties that are barely visible under the hem of the shirt.

My mouth salivates as I flip through page after page of pictures. Some she's almost fully clothed, posing in the cubby of my locker, while others she is completely naked, only covering herself by strategically posing.

Too quickly, I'm at the end.

The last picture features Eleanor laying bare as the day she was born on the soft grass of the soccer pitch. Her hair is feathered out around her in a red halo of curls. Legs straight up in the air and crossed at the ankles, arms outstretched to her sides, and breasts fully on display.

My cock chooses this moment to reappear after hiding inside my body like a turtle tucked in its shell since the second it felt Cecelia's lips on mine.

Again and again, I page through the book, staring at every detail of her body and face. I study every single molecule that makes up her being, afraid that if I look away for even a nanosecond, that I'll miss a minute detail of her soul.

I need to see her–need her in my arms more than I need my next breath and need her back in my bed more than I need to wake tomorrow morning.

How will I ever get her to understand that what she thinks she saw wasn't reality–that she belongs to me and me to her, and that without her, I am but a shell of the man I am when I am with her?

Desperately in need of another drink, I clutch the album to my chest and trudge back to the kitchen. Not bothering to put the book down, I pour another glass, slamming it down before emptying the rest of the bottle into the crystal tumbler.

It may be because of the alcohol coursing through my system or from pure desperation, but I find myself Googling my name–something I never do–looking for the name of the gossip site that has been spreading false information about my alleged rela-tionship with Cecilia.

My entire relationship with Eleanor flashes in front of me through stories and articles, pictures and quotes. Candids from our days at Disney, posed photos from various events, even one of her leaving my house. I recall the yellow sundress she's wearing in that one and smile, knowing it was the first night she stayed in my arms.

At the bottom of one press release, I find contact information for the writer, if you can even call them a writer with the types of shit they post on the daily. And despite it being almost one in the morning on a Sunday, I find myself dialing the numbering, drumming on the kitchen counter while I count the rings.

Several tense moments later, the other end of the line connects, a groggy voice answering. "You've reached Shelby with Gossip Nation Online. This better be good, or I'll be pissed you woke me."

Before I can reconsider, I answer, "This is Jensen West and I want to talk to you–on the record."

The woman's voice audibly picks up, all traces of sleep gone. "Mr. West, I would love to sit down with you for an exclusive. When would be a good time to meet?"

"Now," I all but growl, ready to get my woman back. "I can be at Joe's Diner in half an hour."

"Make it forty-five, and you've got yourself a deal."

I quickly agree before hanging up the phone. I stumble to my room, pulling on clean clothing. Realizing I'm not in any shape to drive, I call an Uber before locking my front door where I wait for my driver on the small front porch.

It's time to get my woman back.

And nothing is going to stop me.

JENSEN WEST SETS THE RECORD STRAIGHT.

Gossip Nation: For Immediate Release

The professional athlete gives a full exclusive to Gossip Nation's own Shelby Johnson.

San Diego, CA, November 7- In an unprecedented move, notorious playboy, Jensen West, has reached out to clear the air regarding his alleged reconciliation with Cecelia Van Hutchinson.

Jensen West is quoted as saying, "I look forward to setting the record straight and cannot wait for the truth to be spoken any longer."

For the full story, visit our website.

END RELEASE

So maybe it wasn't the best idea to sit down with a gossip website reporter at nearly two in the morning without first running it by my agent. But these were desperate times, and surely you know how the old saying goes.

Shelby Johnson sits across from me, picking at a plate of fries while jotting notes down in an old school memo pad as I rattle on. It's the type you'd expect to see a reporter in the 1950's using on some made for television mini-series. The pen scratches across the paper, almost echoing through the quiet diner.

She's a beautiful woman, chestnut brown hair that hangs down to her shoulders and big doe eyes that show no signs of being awoken in the middle of the night for an impromptu meeting. At a previous time in my life, I would have tried to take her home with me for the night–for only one night–but that was before Eleanor. Now, she's the only woman I ever want in my bed again.

"So, what you're saying is that you and Cecelia are *not* together? Is that correct?" Her voice is raspy, sounding like someone much older who has a two-pack-a-day habit, but no smell of stale smoke clings to her or her clothing.

I pick at my own plate–a greasy burger, chips, and extra pickle spears–but I'm too anxious to eat much of anything.

Instead, I push it around while answering her question. "That is absolutely what I'm saying."

Ready to lay everything on the line to get Eleanor back in my life, I start at the beginning of our story, leaving out the juicy details of our first meeting. I tell her about the initial iciness between us, about the pranks we played on each other, and the way we grew closer after our bus trip to Los Angeles. We speak candidly with one another, me sharing with Shelby a bit about my past and about my family. I answer questions about my years playing football, my plans for the future, and what my expectations are for the remainder of the season with Sol. She's easy to talk to, and I quickly see why she is good at her job. Being able to put someone at ease enough for them to drop their defenses is no small task, but for Shelby, it seems to come easily.

Overall, we talk for almost two hours. Her scribbling in her notebook the entire time, me answering each and every question she asks with honesty and full transparency.

While I've conducted many interviews over the years, this is the first one I have actively pursued, the first one I've desperately needed to cement my future. Because I could lose it all tomorrow–soccer, the money, the notoriety–but I absolutely cannot lose Eleanor for good.

She's changed me for the better, made me see a different side of myself–a side worth more than just my dwindling playing career, a side worthy of love and companionship. And I'll be damned if I lose that because some jealous woman tried to come between us.

Shelby and I end our night outside the dinner with a handshake before we go our separate ways. She's promised to have a full article up on the website by the time training is finished tomorrow, and I know once it hits, news will travel to Eleanor quickly.

The team closely monitors all the players, receiving notifications when any of us are mentioned online. Standard practice, though it may seem odd to outsiders. It's used to make sure we aren't tarnishing the reputation of the team and the league, that we aren't getting into any trouble, but this time, it's going to be used for good.

Before I round the corner to the parking lot, I hear Shelby's husky voice call out my name. I turn to face her, and she flashes me a wide grin. "When you win your girl back, I better get the first exclusive!"

I can't help but smile as I reach my car, finally feeling a small bit of hope.

I HAVE. NEVER BEEN. SO TIRED. IN. MY. LIFE.

Granted, I used to be able to party with the best of them, staying up till the wee hours of the morning and arriving at training on time like it was no big deal. Clearly, I'm nowhere near as young as I used to be.

Almost late, I jog through the door into the locker room, quickly change, and head out to the training grounds where most of the team is already practicing. Across the pitch, I see Eleanor, and my chest tightens almost to the point of pain.

Her head is thrown back as she laughs at something, and I find myself jealous of the laugh escaping her lips–jealous that it has the pleasure of touching her skin while I have been pushed to the sidelines, forced to stay away from the one taste that gives me life.

I want nothing more than to stride across the pitch, to press my mouth to hers. I want to push her to her knees and force her to take me in her mouth as punishment for forcing me out of her life just as much as I want to pull her into a crushing embrace and apologize for something I wasn't even the cause of.

Lining up with the majority of guys, we take turns taking

shots on the net, each of us trying to sneak balls past our keepers as they try equally as hard to keep the ball out of the back of the net. All the while, I keep one eye on Eleanor as she works with a smaller group on the opposite side of the pitch.

On my fourth, maybe fifth, attempt against the keeper, I notice Eleanor packing up equipment, making her way around the edge of the pitch and back towards the locker rooms. I sink the ball to the back of the net, stepping aside for my teammates to continue just as she passes behind the same net we're taking shots on.

She steps out from behind the net, one step, two steps, and on her third step, a wide kicked ball careens towards her, knocking into the side of her head before any of us can call out in warning.

The items she had stacked between her arms tumble to the ground only a nanosecond before she does. I'm already running towards her as Cole calls out to the team medic, who is quickly at my side as I kneel on the grass next to her. Coach is close behind, coming to kneel with the rest of us as Eleanor's green eyes flutter open.

Wide-eyed, she looks around at the three of us, dazed. "Wha...what happened?"

She tries to stand but quickly teeters back over. This time, I'm right there, catching her before she can tumble back to the ground. "You took a ball to the noggin, Love."

The medic moves in, assessing her condition with a small flashlight and checking her responses as she follows his finger in different patterns. Already, a nasty goose egg is forming on her flawless skin, showing where the ball made direct contact while barely missing her temple. "Safe to say you've got a concussion, Elle. You're going to need someone to stay with you for the next twenty-four to forty-eight hours."

Eleanor goes to protest, but I stop her before she can fully open her mouth. "She'll stay with me."

Both her and Coach's eyes look to me, and while hers are glassy and etched in confusion, Coach's are plagued with concern. As well as the rest of the team, Coach knows exactly what has transpired between us. He's noted my mood swings, my outbursts, and I know he doesn't appreciate them. He addresses Eleanor directly. "Is that okay with you?"

She locks her eyes on me the best she can after taking a ball to the head that had been traveling upwards of sixty miles per hour. Her voice is small and pained when she responds, nothing like the normally deeper timbre she emits. "Yes, that is okay with me."

Coach gives her a reassuring nod before turning to me. "West, you're excused for the rest of the day. Get her home safe, and keep us updated on any changes in her condition."

I can't help but reach out and place a hand on his shoulder, a silent understanding that I will take care of her. And I will because she is mine to take care of. She is mine to cherish and worship, and while a concussion wasn't the way I had planned for our reunion to start, I won't pass up this opportunity to show her exactly what she means to me.

Before she can try to stand on wobbly feet again, I scoop her up into my arms, holding her tight against my chest. I relish in the feeling of her own arms as they loop around my neck, and while it may only be because she is feeling off-kilter, I soak in the contact between our bodies on the entire walk to the locker room.

Foregoing a shower, I quickly change while Eleanor sits cautiously on a bench that runs down the center of the room. "Stay right here, baby. I'll get your bag from your desk."

She doesn't answer, just stares straight ahead, and I'm not sure if it's from the ball to the head or because she is apprehensive about being alone with me after two long and grueling weeks of being apart.

Gingerly, we make it to my car. Once she is seated, I reach

around her torso, fastening her safety belt into place. My fingers linger for a moment longer than necessary. They itch to touch her, to run through her hair and caress her soft skin. Instead, I settle for tucking one lone curl behind her ear before closing the door and walking around to the driver's side.

We don't talk on the entire drive to my house, and when we arrive, Eleanor opens the car door, one foot stepping onto the driveway before I stop her. She's fragile right now, and even if she is capable of making it inside on her own, I don't want her to. She needs to be in my arms, or maybe it's me that needs to be in hers.

With great care, I lead her to the couch, helping her to lower herself to the cushions below. "I'll get you something to change into."

She gives me a small yet weak smile. "Thank you."

I return a few minutes later, an old Sol tee and sweatpants in hand. Offering to help her to the bathroom to change, she surprises me with a small laugh. "It isn't like you haven't seen me naked before."

Eleanor peels her team polo over her head, wincing when the fabric brushes the hardened skin of her bruise. Quickly, I'm at her side, helping to guide her the rest of the way. She lets me help, lets me unclasp her bra and slide it down her arms before I delicately place my old tee over her head, guiding her arms through the holes. Lifting her ass from the couch, she allows me to shimmy her pants down her legs, depositing them on the floor at her feet. We've been silent the entire time, but when I bring my sweatpants up to her, she swats them away before speaking. "Too sleepy for pants. Can I just stay like this?"

I point to the pillow at the edge of the couch, instructing her to place her head on the soft surface. Grabbing a blanket from the back of the couch, I drape it over her body before walking to the windows, closing the blinds. When the daylight is sufficiently obscured from the room, I return to the couch, kneeling at her side. "You scared the absolute shit out of me, Eleanor."

Her eyes are heavy, and I know it's the concussion taking hold of her body. "Close your eyes and get some sleep. I have to wake you every few hours to check on you, but today especially, it's imperative that you get lots of rest."

She listens to my request without putting up a fight, closing her eyes and drifting off to sleep within minutes. I stay on the floor, just watching her breathe, so happy to have her back in my home.

When I'm sure she's truly asleep, I lean over her, brushing the lightest kiss to her forehead before whispering to her, even though I know she won't hear it. "I love you, Eleanor, and I'll do whatever it takes to prove that to you."

COACH BIGSBY ENDURES TRAINING MISHAP.

Soccer Daily Online: For Immediate Release

Although common among players, Bigsby's concussion is the first for Sol's coaching staff.

San Diego, CA, November 8- During a recent early morning practice, conditioning coach, Eleanor Bigsby, suffered a concussion after being hit in the head with a wayward ball. Team sources say the twenty-two-year-old was escorted from the pitch in the arms of Jensen West. The pair was seen leaving together shortly after the incident.

Coach James Calder is quoted as saying, "I will not comment on our coach or player's personal lives. However, I will say that while Coach Bigsby did sustain a concussion during practice, she is doing well and is being carefully monitored. Our team's health and safety is our top priority, and that extends to our coaching team as well."

END RELEASE

My head is pounding when I wake, and I'm momentarily confused when I sit, looking around at my surroundings. It comes back to me when I look to the left, finding Jensen curled up on a recliner, a blanket over his body. The television is on, though the volume is muted, some sports show playing on the screen.

I don't remember the ball hitting my head, but reaching up to feel the large bump, I know that's exactly what happened.

What I do remember though, is Jensen. His strong arms as he caught me when I nearly fell to the ground a second time, those same arms around me as he cradled me and carried me to the locker room, how delicately he buckled me into his car as if I were a prized possession he was afraid to lose.

It's still light, though curtains block out much of the sun. I'm desperate for water and something to numb the constant throbbing in my skull. Pushing the light blanket that Jensen draped over me to the couch, I go to stand but am stopped when I see a clear glass and two tablets on the coffee table.

Without hesitation, I pick up the tablets and pop them into my mouth before taking long sips from the glass to wash them down. Setting the now empty glass on the table, my eye flicks to the only other item on the bare table.

The photo album I had made for him.

I suck in a shuddering breath, wondering what it means.

He didn't throw it out, didn't toss it in a drawer or the back of a closet. Does that mean that Cecelia has seen it? Has she been in his house at all over the past two weeks? And if they are actually together, why is the album so prominently on display?

Rising to my feet, I quietly plod to the bathroom, doing my best not to disturb Jensen. Glancing at the clock over the stove on my way, I surmise that I've been asleep for about two hours. Regardless, it feels like I could sleep for the next three days without waking.

I check out the bump on my head and yikes...it's not pretty. Slightly black and blue, if I look close enough, I swear I can make out the pattern of the ball in the exact place it struck me.

The only thing more ridiculous than the knot on my head is the way I look in Jensen's too small for me tee and underwear I specifically reserve for work. The shirt is old and thin, my nipples showing through the fabric, while my underwear is plain cotton and surely has stains on them somewhere from period mishaps of months gone by.

Taking the opportunity while in the bathroom, I splash a little cold water on my face, finally feeling a bit more alert. If I could only do something about the ridiculous get-up I'm currently sporting.

I return to the living room, falling back into a cocoon of warmth under the blanket. Reaching down to my bag that is on the floor next to me, I quietly dig around until I find my cell, knowing that by now, my dad has certainly heard about my training mishap. What I'm not prepared for is the absolute onslaught of messages that light up across my phone as I tap on the screen to illuminate it.

Texts from my entire family clog my inbox along with messages from Ophelia, Coach James and Coach Terry, Cole, and almost every other player from the team. I have get well messages, texts full of helpful tips and tricks for recovery, and the typical playful messages from Ophelia featuring scantily clad pictures of male doctors that bring a smile to my face. In the mix are GIFs of people getting hit in the head by various objects, a few frantic texts and calls from my mother demanding I call her as soon as possible, and even one from Rochelle in marketing who must have heard about the incident through the not-so-subtle grapevine that is my work best friend.

Not wanting to wake Jensen but knowing if I don't talk to my mom soon that she is likely to call the cops to file a missing person's report, I sneak out onto the back patio, phone clutched in my hand. Thankful for the tall palms and thick pittosporum bushes surrounding the property, I don't have to worry about covering up, choosing to come out in nothing but Jensen's tee and my panties. While it's too late in the season for the shrubs to bloom, I can almost smell what will be their fragrant flowers–reminiscent of orange blossoms–when the spring rolls around. I walk to the edge of the property, peering over the wooden gate that leads down several steps to the sand below.

My mother picks up before the first ring is even finished.

"Eleanor Grace Bigsby, I have been trying to contact you for *hours*! Where on God's green earth are you? Are you okay? How is your head? You really should go to the hospital; you could be in need a CT scan. You know what I always say, Eleanor; it is better to be safe than sorry."

Ahh, my mother, the original helicopter parent.

Seriously. Growing up under Bethany Bigsby's roof was always an adventure. While my dad was often out of the state for work, my mom played the role of the quintessential stay-at-home mother. She was head of the PTA for all four of her children, was at every team practice and game, almost always had a home-cooked meal on the table, and even chaperoned our school dances. That last one, I'm pretty sure was only so that she could keep an eye on us, making sure we stayed a proper distance between our dancing partners or that we didn't sneak off to drink in the bathroom.

While it was overbearing at times, it was also what helped my sister and I to become so close. I can't count the times we covered for one another while the other snuck out on a date or out to a party with friends.

Needless to say, my mother has not gotten better as her children aged.

"Mom, I'm okay. It's just a little concussion."

"Don't be silly, dear; you can't be too cautious. Now tell me where you are. You really should be home so I can take care of you."

I sigh into the receiver. If my mother had her way, all four of us kids would live with her for the rest of our lives. Even with Jeff married and Marc in a long-term partnership with his college sweetheart, she'd still prefer to have them under her roof.

"I promise, I am okay. The team medic checked me out, and I have someone taking good care of me. If there are any changes, I will go to the emergency room right away."

It's my mom's turn to sigh. As she does, I hear the door to the patio snick open and peer behind me to see Jensen making his way tentatively toward where I am standing at the edge of the property. "Ellie, baby girl," a smile tugs at my lips at my childhood nickname, "I just worry about you, okay? You're a grown woman in this big, giant world, so different from the little girl I fell in love with at first sight all those years ago. I just...I just always want the best for you because you deserve it. I never want to see you hurting–not from a friend, or a man, or even a silly little soccer ball."

That makes me feel sentimental while making me giggle at the same time.

"I'm so lucky to have you for my mom," I say. And I truly mean it.

If I couldn't have my birth mother in my life, there is absolutely no one else I would want to have the role of mother than Bethany Bigsby–hovering and all. She exudes the definition of love, fiercely protecting her family like the proud mama bear she is.

Promising her I'll call her again in the morning, or if there is any change in my condition, I tell her how much I love her before saying goodbye as tears form in my eyes.

For a girl who isn't overly emotional, I have a hard time keeping the tears from spilling over, but between seeing my photo album on Jensen's coffee table and my talk with my mom, I'm a total wreck. I blame the concussion.

I turn, facing Jensen for the first time since he appeared behind me. Lip quivering, I stare into his blue eyes, the same color as the blue flax that bloom throughout the city. They're so full of hope, of tenderness, of love–but also of pain and longing.

He reaches out for me, but pauses mere inches away. When he speaks, his voice quakes with emotion, and it pulls at my already tattered heart. "I was so damn worried about you, so scared you were seriously hurt. Eleanor, if something happened to you, I don't know what I would do, don't know how I would go on."

I give him a small, reassuring smile as I tease, "Now you sound like my mom."

His expression doesn't change, the furrow between his brow deepening. Almost pleading, he asks, "Please, can I hug you?"

I don't know where we stand or what comes next for us, but in this moment, I need his arms around me just as much as he seems to need mine around him. I step into his arms, sliding mine around his strong back as the tears really start to fall. Soaking his shirt, we stand for several minutes, lost in the strength we give one another.

We don't need words right now. Don't need false promises of tomorrow or wild nights of passion. We simply need the connection we feel when our arms are around each other. It's powerful, that feeling. And it's a feeling I never want to end.

"Eleanor," he presses the lightest kiss to the top of my head, and I can tell he is as hesitant to let go of me as I am of him, "I need to show you something."

ONE-ON-ONE WITH JENSEN WEST.

Gossip Nation: For Immediate Release

The notoriously silent celeb sits down for a one-on-one conversation with Gossip Nation's own Shelby Johnson. Full story below.

San Diego, CA, November 8- As a reporter, when your phone rings at almost two in the morning, you answer. Many times, it's for nothing, but every once in a blue moon, one of those middle-of-the-night phone calls turns out to be worth waking up for.

Imagine my surprise when one of those recent late-night telephone calls turned out to be none other than San Diego Sol's Jensen West. As much as the phone call surprised me, I was even more shocked when he asked me to meet at a downtown diner that very same morning.

That's how I found myself across from Jensen, eating greasy diner food and drinking cups of coffee until the sun was almost peeking from behind the clouds.

But perhaps the biggest surprise of all, Jensen West has a lot to say, and he wants you to hear it.

Keep reading for our full interview.

ONE-ON-ONE WITH JENSEN WEST.

Gossip Nation: For Immediate Release

Shelby: You've been notorious for quite a few things over the years. A closed-lipped man who keeps most things to himself, a two-time Golden Boot winner, salacious playboy, and occasional hot-head. Do you find that you have been accurately portrayed by the media?

Jensen: I think that every rumor starts with some morsel of truth, even if it is a truth we don't see at the time. There have definitely been times I've let my temper get the best of me, and I'm sure some of the playboy image comes from a place of truth. I mean, I certainly had a lot of fun in my younger years. But at the same time, there are many things I think the media has gotten wrong about me as well. I don't often speak about my family—one, because it can be a source of pain, and two, because I am fiercely protective of the people I love, and I desperately wish to protect them from the media.

Shelby: You've been under that media scrutiny since you were very young. Do you think it has shaped you into the person you are today?

Jensen: Absolutely. I learned from a young age that almost everything that comes out of my mouth will be twisted in one way or another. More times than not, those words do not benefit me, but instead the person on the other end of the conversation. It doesn't matter if that has been in professional relationships, romantic relationships, or friendships. It has happened more times that I care to count, and at some point, I became guarded, locking feelings away from the people that were most important to me.

Shelby: I can understand that. The feelings of animosity that comes with the territory. It's certainly something that gives people in my profession a bad reputation. I'm sincerely apologetic for any incorrect information I may have published in the past.

ONE-ON-ONE WITH JENSEN WEST.

Gossip Nation: For Immediate Release

Jensen: Thank you. Up until very recently, I don't know that I would have been mature enough to accept that apology. I don't know that I would have wanted to accept it.

Shelby: So, tell me Jensen, what changed?

Jensen: I met a woman.

Shelby: Ah, it's always a woman. Isn't it?

Jensen: I suppose it is. But this one, she's different than the rest.

Shelby: From chatting with you today, is it safe to assume that woman is not Cecelia Van Hutchinson?

Jensen: That would absolutely be the correct assumption.

Shelby: And this woman, would it be a particular red-headed stunner that you were spotted with several times over the last several months?

Jensen: You've assumed correctly again.

Shelby: Tell me, what is it about her that makes her different?

Jensen: Eleanor and I did not start off on the greatest terms. At the beginning of the season, I was in a very rough spot mentally and emotionally. I had been fighting with myself over my age and the limited playing time I had left, with the next steps I would take, and what my future held for me. She swept into the locker room, young and beautiful, and utterly irritating with how she got under my skin. I tried desperately to push her away, but with everything I threw at her, she threw it right back at me.

ONE-ON-ONE WITH JENSEN WEST.

Gossip Nation: For Immediate Release

Shelby: Can you go into greater detail about that?

Jensen: If we had been working in a traditional office, you would say we had our own Office Warsgoing on. Everything from scaring each other by jumping out of hidden places to hiding things from one another.

Shelby: It certainly sounds like you've met your match in Eleanor Bigsby.

Jensen: I have. Or, I had.

Shelby: Will you tell me about what happened between the two of you?

Jensen: Seeing as how you have written several press releases about the recent events, I'm sure you already know. But to give you the CliffsNotes, a certain social media influencer turned model turned wannabe pop star reappeared in my life, and not for good.

Shelby: Cecelia Van Hutchinson?

Jensen: We briefly dated, if you could even call it that, a bit over a year ago before going our separate ways. I knew she was not satisfied with our breakup when it happened but never expected that she would sabotage my relationship with Eleanor due to her own jealousy. When she approached me at Sol in the Park a few weeks ago, I was not excited to see her. I did not want to reconcile with her then, and I certainly do not wish to reconcile with her now. Her advances at the event were unwanted and not returned on my end. Unfortunately, Cecelia was busy throwing herself at me, and my true love witnessed the event. She did it because she knew it would play into Eleanor's insecurities and that it would tear us apart. Her plan worked, and it drove us apart.

ONE-ON-ONE WITH JENSEN WEST.

Gossip Nation: For Immediate Release

Shelby: I know you just said a whole lot there, Jensen, but the one thing that stuck out was that you said she tore you apart from your true love?

Jensen: That is correct, Shelby. I've done a lot of stupid things in my life. I've fucked up more times than I care to admit. Oh, shit, am I allowed to say fucked up? Fuck, I just said it again.

Shelby: You're fine, go ahead.

Jensen: Anyway, through all the shit I've done and been unsure of, there is one thing that I am unequivocally sure of and that is that I am one-hundred-percent in love with Eleanor Bigsby.

Shelby: So, where do you go from here?

Jensen: As I grow older, I've learned that the best thing you can do is talk. I know that might sound silly coming from someone who has been as tightlipped as I have been over the years, but in this scenario, I refuse to lose the love of my life because of a misunderstanding, because of a situation we were both thrust into where neither of us were wrong, but we saw what was happening from two different angles and both acted accordingly.

Shelby: Wise advice.

Jensen: And if talking doesn't work, I'm not above groveling.

Shelby: Any last parting words you'd like to say?

Jensen: If there was anything I wish I could convey to Eleanor, it's how much she changed my life for the better. She's truly made me a better man, made me see my own worth is in more than what I can do on the pitch. I know I'm not the easiest man to love, but if she can find it in her heart to love me, I'll fucking worship her for the rest of our lives because there is nothing she deserves more.

Say what you want about Jensen West. Chances are, he won't care, but one thing is for sure. After sitting down to chat with the soccer stud, one more word that will soon be used to describe him is romantic.

From everyone here at Gossip Nation, we wish Jensen the best in not only his career but in his personal life as well.

END RELEASE

I SEARCH JENSEN'S FACE, studying every emotion that radiates from his body. The apprehension and vulnerability are like none I've ever seen from him before. It both makes my heart soar and break at the same time.

"You...love me?" I finally manage to ask after a full minute of silence.

Sitting in the chair behind his desk, in the office where he made me cum with the help of his best friend while giving me power I never knew I lacked, I have just read the online exclusive Jensen gave to Gossip Nation. For maybe the first time in my life, I am almost completely speechless.

Stepping around the desk, he gently spins the chair until I am facing him before sinking to his knees on the ground in front of me. "So fucking much, Eleanor. Probably since the first day of training when your tiny, little palm connected with the side of my face." He reaches up with one hand, gently cupping my cheek. "God, I knew you were beautiful that night at the club, the things you did with your body—the things you let me do to you. But that day at training, you stood up to me, refused to take shit from me, and it was the sexiest fucking thing I have ever seen in my entire life. You've pushed me since day one, challenged me, fucking driven me crazy, and shown me what a relationship can be with the right person.

"Everything I said to that reporter, every last word, it's all true. I can't fucking lose you because, at my core, I'm fucking nothing without you. With you by my side, I've learned to not be afraid of what the future holds because it doesn't matter what comes next in my career. It only matters that you're there with me."

Pushing back in the chair, I move to the ground, too, kneeling in front of where he dropped. I need to be closer to him. Need to place my hands on his skin, still afraid that he's a desert mirage that will disappear if I get too close.

Tears fall from my eyes for the second time today, and when I lock eyes with Jensen, I notice his eyes have gone glassy as well. Reluctantly, I reach up to his face, wiping away the lone tear that had streaked down his face.

"Please, say something, Princess. Anything at all, I just need you to say something."

My breathing is uneven and shaky as I wipe at my own tears. I try to speak but can't form a coherent sentence. In one of probably the least sexy moves ever, I start to laugh uncontrollably, overwhelmed by the emotions not only coursing through my body, but coursing between Jensen and myself as well. They swirl around us like a tornado, dropping love, lust, adoration, longing, and so many other feels throughout the small office.

Finally, I'm able to squeak out words between the fits of laughter that have begun to flow between us. "You really love me? Really want to be with me?"

He takes my hands in his. "I've never wanted anything more in my life."

"I've missed you so much, been so miserable without you. I'm so, so, *so* sorry that I didn't believe you, that I didn't stop to listen to you because it would have saved us both two weeks of hell." I sob–full on body heaving sobs–as he pulls me into his arms. My own immediately wrap around his torso, holding onto him with enough force to require the jaws of life to pry me from his body.

"Shhhhh, Princess, it's okay. I'm here now; we're here now. Together."

"I've never been in love before, and you may think it's hard, but loving you is the easiest thing I've ever done, Jensen. You think that you're nothing without me, that I've changed your life, but God, you have no idea what you've done for me.

"You've given me confidence, shown me how to love myself and my body. Hell, you made me love *soccer,* for Christ's sake."

His hands come up to tangle in my hair. Gently, he uses my curls to tug me away from his body. "Fuck, baby, I need to kiss you right now."

Not waiting for a response, his lips descend on mine in a kiss unlike any we've ever shared. It's slow and sensual, like he's exploring me again for the first time while deciding how far he can push me. He licks at the seam of my lips, and I willfully open to him, allowing his tongue to dance with mine in languid strokes. His kisses elicit moans from deep within my soul, and he gladly drinks them down while continuing to lick into my mouth.

We pull apart, breathless and panting. "You were fucking made for me, Eleanor. Your luscious body and killer curves, your brilliant mind and sexy as hell brain–Goddamn, I want every single piece of you."

"You have me–all of me. I'm all yours, for as long as you'll have me."

"Forever, baby. I'll need you forever."

His hands trail and up and down my back, sneaking under the thin fabric of his old t-shirt I'm wearing while sending goosebumps over my flesh. We're both still on our knees, my head pressed against his chest. "I was hoping and praying to a God I'm not even sure exists that you would come back to me. All I want to do is take you bed right now, tear that shirt right down the middle, and make you cum over and over again until you're a sobbing, sloppy, wet mess. But as badly as I need in that tight little cunt of yours, I need you to heal first. So now, I'm going to carry you to my bed, which I hope will soon become our bed when you agree to move in with me, and then we're going to order delivery, stuff ourselves full, put some nonsense television on a nice low volume, and nap together tangled in each other's arms."

For a brief moment, I had all but forgotten about my concussion, forgotten about what brought me back to Jensen's today. His dirty words alone already have me clenching my thighs in anticipation, and I'm about to interject and tell him that I'm fine when what he said finally registers. "Wait...what did you say?"

"That I'm going to carry you to bed."

"No, after that..."

"We're going to order delivery, eat, and nap?"

"Before that."

"That I want to turn *my* house into *our* home?"

I nod. "Yep, that's the part. You want me to move into your house?"

"Baby, it hasn't been just my house since the first night you decided to give me a chance and had dinner here with me. I've been dreaming of having you here with me every day, but if you think it's too soon..."

"No!" I blurt it out. "It's not too soon! I want mornings with you where we make pancakes together, and you laugh at how messy I am with the batter. I want weekends with you where we float in the pool and have parties with our friends, and nights where we take baths together in that giant tub where you let me wash your hair and massage your back after a hard day at training."

"Absolute. Utter. Perfection," he coos in my ear.

Finally, we make our way from the floor back to our feet before Jensen scoops me up, making good on his promise to carry me to bed. He sets me under the covers before disappearing to the bathroom, only to return with a glass of water and more pain relievers. "Drink up, Love. Then close your eyes, and I'll order us food. You're going to need a few days of rest, but I'll be next to you the entire time."

Graciously, I accept the water, finishing the glass in a few large gulps before placing my head on the oversized pillows at the head of the bed. Jensen crawls into bed next to me, and it's the most natural feeling in the world–laying in bed with someone I thought I was destined to hate, concussed, and half-naked.

I wouldn't change for the world.

I wouldn't change *him* for the world.

SAN DIEGO SOL ADVANCES TO FINAL.

Soccer Daily Online: For Immediate Release

After a dismal finish last season, Sol has done a full 180 to advance to the MLS final.

San Diego, CA, November 16- A true underdog story, San Diego Sol is looking to create magic with their appearance in the upcoming MLS final. In the 26-year history of the sport in America, only one other team has been able to move from second to last place and advance to win the cup the following year.

Coach James Calder is quoted as saying, "We want to win; that's always our goal. But regardless of the outcome, I am incredibly proud of what our team has accomplished and look forward to how our team will continue to grow in the future. I truly believe that San Diego can become the next hub for soccer in the United States, and I am excited to be part of that process."

END RELEASE

Eleanor is on the mattress, ass in the air while her chest is pressed to the bed. We might have lost our final match of the season a few months ago, not winning the trophy, but she's the real prize anyway. Yeah, I'm bummed, but she's definitely helping to make up for it.

"Jensen, please!" she screams into the mattress, trying to escape the sensation of the vibrator I've been teasing her clit with for the past ten minutes. Every single time she is about to cum, I pull it away, teasing her thighs, up and down her spine, and even the sensitive skin of her asshole.

"What's wrong, Love? Is it too much for you?"

"YES!" she cries out.

I land a hand on her ass cheek. "Do you want me to stop?"

Through a whimper, she manages to sneak out a, "No, please no."

Although she is mostly healed from her concussion, I've still been gentler with her than I normally am. I'm not mad about it though; it's giving me an entirely new way to play with and appreciate her body.

I bring the vibe back to her cunt, teasing it through her folds, over her slick pussy, but never quite pushing it to the little bundle of nerves that will send her over the edge. "Remember that day you forced the team to hike the steps?"

She sucks in a shaky breath. "Yes."

I laugh mischievously. "You got so fucking pissed at me when I blurted out that you were a masochist, but you really are, aren't you? You love when I tease you with a little bit of pain, don't you, Love?"

I bring my palm down on her ass again, hard enough that she yelps before she moans at the sensation it sends ricocheting through her body. "God, yes."

Using the same hand, I slide my fingers through her soaking wet pussy before spreading the wetness up her ass. All the while, I continue to tease her with the gentle vibrations of the toy. One finger probes at her asshole, slowly sliding into her most sacred place. She's not ready to take all of me there yet, but we've recently started prepping, stretching her with various plugs. I can't wait for the day I can push past that muscle, sliding into her tight, virgin ass.

"And you like when I humiliate you, too, don't you, my little cum slut?" Ever so gently, I drag the vibrator over her clit. "You're so beautiful when you whimper for me, Eleanor. Do you think I should let you cum now?"

"Daddy, please!"

I'm not exactly sure when she started calling me Daddy–all I know is it makes me absolutely fucking feral. Last week, while at dinner, I asked her between courses if she wanted dessert. When she slid over next to me, and whispered, "Yes, Daddy," into my ear at the same time she slid her hand up my thigh and grabbed my cock, I almost exploded. I certainly had dessert; I just don't think Eleanor expected it would be her on the menu. Before we could even leave the restaurant, I pulled her into the bathroom and locked the door before hauling her onto the counter, tearing her panties from her body, and feasting on her delectable cunt.

"Oh, little girl..." I slide the vibe to her clit, holding it there for one, two, three seconds before pulling it away. She whines like a lost little puppy, and if my cock wasn't already rock hard, the sound would have gone straight to my dick. "You can ask your Daddy better than that, can't you?"

Slick juices coat her thighs, and from my place on the mattress, I have the most perfect view of her cunt, glistening with need. There is a growing wet spot on the mattress below her from where she drips, and even though her face is pressed deep into the mattress, I can hear a sob as it escapes her mouth. Christ, I love when she is a mess for me. I love that she knows she can ask me to stop at any time, and I will, but that she never asks, taking everything I give her with wanton appreciation. We've talked about safe words, limits, turn ons and offs. Safe to say while we have a safe word, Eleanor doesn't have any fucking hard limits and never chooses to use her chosen word.

I'm a lucky fucking man.

"Daddy, may I please cum for you?"

"Mmmm...you are such a good little cum slut for me, Eleanor. You turn your Daddy on, don't you?" I lightly hold the vibrator to her clit, feeling her writhe against it. "You're going to cum for me, Princess. You're going to cum with this toy pressed against your sensitive little clit, and then when you're laying in a pile of your own arousal, I'm going to fuck you until I cum deep inside that perfect, pink pussy. Would you like that?"

"Yessss," she hisses out as I press harder against her. "Please, please let me cum!"

Without warning, I press the button on the side of the toy, turning it up one speed. Eleanor screams so loud at the sensation that I'm sure the neighbors down the beach consider calling the police, afraid I'm tormenting the poor woman. Her hips buck against the toy as her orgasm starts, and as she writhes her way through wave after wave of her orgasm, liquid pools on the mattress beneath her. I slap her pussy with an open palm as juices continue to flow from her cunt, splashing her warm arousal onto the inside of her thigh, down her stomach, and even onto my own chest. "Dirty girl–making a mess and squirting all over the sheets."

She turns her head to the side, and I see the tears running down her face, beautiful black streaks all over her cheeks. Eleanor told me she had a surprise for me today, and when I asked what it was, she tossed a tube of mascara at me–the deepest black color that isn't waterproof. Guaranteed to smear, just how we both like it.

As Eleanor comes down from riding her high, her body trembles, the aftershocks of her orgasms coursing through her body. But the entire time, as she shakes and sways, she holds that perfectly round ass in the air, waiting for me to slide into her pussy from behind.

Already naked, I climb behind her on the mattress, not caring that I'm kneeling in her juices that have spilled all over our bed. She's wet, so fucking slippery for me, but even if she wasn't, I'd be pounding into her to the hilt in one stroke anyway. My girl likes the bite of pain, relishes in it, and sometimes, she even begs for it.

I fuck into her pussy over and over, and the entire time I do, she sobs. She does this sometimes, and I always ask if I should stop, but she always insists I keep going, that it is a good cry, a cathartic cry. Somewhere deep inside, I understand it, and beyond anything else, I want to give her what she needs.

Her pussy clenches around my cock, sending me quickly to the edge. The all too familiar tingle starts at the base of my spine, slowly spreading to my cock. Still I continue to slam into her tight cunt again and again and again. "Where do you want me to cum, Princess?"

I love to give her the choice of where I finish, empowering her to choose what she's in the mood for while allowing me to use her body as a vessel. Sometimes it's inside her, other times it's a request for her tits or her face. Today, it's my favorite request of all. "In my mouth–I want to taste you in my mouth."

I groan, sliding out of her cunt, immediately missing the heat of her tight sex. I wrap one hand around my dick, and the other goes to her hair and pulls until her top half is off the mattress and she's turning around to face me. Flat on her back, I straddle her face, pumping my dick hard and fast. I lock my stare on her gorgeous green eyes, made even brighter by the streaks of black marring her perfectly pale cheeks. "Stick out your tongue, baby girl. You take it for me, but don't you dare swallow. I want you to hold my cum in your mouth. Can you do that?"

"Yes."

"Yes, what?"

She smiles up at me through her absolutely wrecked face, a wicked angel sent to rescue me from myself when I needed most to be pulled back from the depths of hell. "Yes, Daddy."

Then her lips part, and she sticks her tongue out in a silent, magnificent offering. I place the tip of my cock against her tongue and allow myself to tumble over the edge of oblivion. Spurts of my arousal hit her tongue, coating the inside of her mouth. I expel so much cum from my cock that it barely fits in her tiny, little mouth, a small trickle escaping from the corner. "You better hold that for me!" I growl, the visceral need to see her claimed growing in me every day.

Finally, my cock is spent, and I look down at the most beautiful site ever. Disheveled and thoroughly dicked, Eleanor looks up at me, mouth still wide open and full of my cum. She's laying in a pool of her own making, her breasts have been mottled with love bites, and as she spreads her legs, I see her cunt is still glistening with desire. I reach between her legs, swiping one digit through her slick pussy, bringing it up to my lips. Her eyes flare as I suck my finger, and her chest heaves with heavy breaths. The entire time she watches, she holds her mouth open to me, allowing me to stare down at my cum as it sits in her filthy mouth.

"Do you want to swallow that now?"

She shakes her head left to right.

"You want to spit it out?"

Again, she shakes her head.

"Well then, baby, you're going to have to show me what you want because I don't know of any other options."

Pushing herself off her back, she shuts her lips, holding her mouth closed. Pushing me backward until I'm now lying on my back, she straddles me, those gorgeous, thick fucking thighs I love so much holding me captive, and with her mouth over mine, she cocks an eyebrow in my direction.

"You dirty fucking woman."

She nods, and of course, I'm so tightly wrapped around her finger that I'd do anything to make her happy. Slightly hesitant, I part my lips as she lowers her head closer to mine. And when there are only a few inches between us, she slowly parts her own lips, allowing my release to dribble from her mouth into mine.

It's a unique taste I've never experienced before. It's the musky and tangy taste of her mixed with the salty release of mine, and it immediately becomes my favorite taste in the world. I'd drink it down every fucking day if it meant watching her like this.

I close my mouth, holding my release in my mouth, and as I go to swallow, Eleanor stalls me by bringing her lips to mine, licking the cum that missed my mouth, tasting it for herself. "You can spit it out."

My eyes holding hers, I take one large gulp, swallowing it down before showing her my tongue, like I so often make her show me. The grin that spreads across her face is contagious, and I find myself smiling back. She leans over me, grinding once, twice, three times over my already hardening cock before dropping to whisper in my ear, "I guess I'm not the only masochist, am I, Daddy?"

I pull her into my arms, wrapping her in the love that radiates from them, needing her body to be as close to mine as humanly possible. "I guess not, baby girl. I guess fucking not."

She sighs, a content, little sound that never fails to make me happy. As she runs tired, clumsy fingers through my hair, she says, "I really am sorry about the final. That ref had it out for us from the beginning, but I know how much it meant to you."

I play with a strand of hair, rolling the curl back and forth between my fingers. "Aye, he certainly wasn't on our side, but truly, it's okay. I've got one more year left on my contract before renegotiations. And besides, as it turns out, after all my years of playing, I'm beginning to think that soccer isn't actually the most beautiful game."

"If not soccer, then what?" she asks, genuine confusion in her voice.

"Ah, Eleanor, the most beautiful game after all, is you."

THE END

ACKNOWLEDGMENTS

Every novel that makes it to publishing is a true collaboration and for me, Beautiful Games really is a story that was a collaborative effort. Of all my books, this one pulls strongly on personal experiences-which parts, I'll leave up to your imagination.

To my other half-who went from being my fiance to my wife during this book-I truly couldn't have done it without you. While my love for the sport of soccer is vast, it is nowhere near as vast as your knowledge on the subject. Thank you, as always, for being my first reader, but also for always being there for me to bounce ideas with, and for this book, to be the person to look at me and say "that's not how it happens in real life." Sorry if the liberties I took with some of the soccer portion of the story drive you crazy. Just kidding, I'm totally not.

My brilliant editor, Tiffany-over the last three books, you've truly become more than an editor. You've become someone I look to for advice, know I can always count on with my crazy questions, and are always so thorough yet kind with your edits. You continually help me to shape my stories into something I am excited to release into the wild.

Cady and Tori, the phenomenal duo of Cruel Ink Editing + Design-from the absolute kick-ass cover of the cheeky Jensen West, to the incredible formatting, the two of you continue to surpass all my expectations of making my words look beautiful. Thank you both for never failing to answer my texts outside of business hours, for answering my gazillion-and-one questions, and for always managing to fit me in at the last minute. I know, I know-I'm the worst.

To my alphas, betas, and every single one of my soccer friends who spent countless hours speculating who Jensen West was based off of-thank you for the laughs, some tears, and endless conversations while I should have been writing.

ABOUT AMITY MALCOM...

Amity Malcom was born in Pennsylvania. She began writing short stories while still in elementary school-including a total page turner about how her mother loved to fish. Her mother does not love to fish and is actually terrified by ocean creatures.

She now resides in Florida with her wife, two completely insane but lovable cats and one neurotic but adorable dog.

When not writing steamy characters and happily ever afters, Amity can be found watching professional soccer, exploring Florida's many theme parks, and campaigning for LGBTQIA+ rights.